under the blue moon

A FIVE DIRECTIONS PRESS BOOK

under
the
blue
moon

joan schweighardt

ISBN-13 978-1947044357

e-ISBN 978-1947044364

Published in the United States of America.

Cover images: Wavy, abstract mountains from iStock.com; paw prints from Shutterstock.com.

Book and cover design by Five Directions Press

Five Directions Press logo designed by Colleen Kelley

Five Directions Press

Lovers don't finally meet somewhere.
They're in each other all along.

—Mawlana Jalal-al-Din Rumi

1

LOLA
absent

The first thing Lola noticed upon impact was that she had lime green paint under her fingernails, and in that instant she couldn't remember why. The second thing was that her car was still in motion even though she was no longer driving it. Her foot was on the brake—hard, in fact—but it wasn't helping because she was moving not forward but sideways. There had been people sitting all along the curb that she was heading into—deranged looking people, she'd been thinking a split second earlier, with wild hair and wide eyes—but now they were all screaming (she assumed they were screaming; their mouths were open, though she couldn't actually hear anything over the horrible screeching noise her car was making, over the pounding in her ears), scurrying to their feet, jumping out of the way.

Her car hit the curb and bounced once before stopping, jerking Lola forward for a second time. Her head didn't hit the steering wheel but bobbed near it, and as her fingers were still clenched there, she noticed the paint under her nails once again. With everything else going on, her awareness of this detail was peripheral at best, but it would come back to haunt her later; it would be there whenever she went over the particulars in her mind.

Her first *conscious* thought was the curb, of course, whether everyone had gotten up off it in time or if there were still some people there, their legs crushed between it and her car. She made herself look in that direction. Her eye fell on the brick building on the other side of the sidewalk. Leaning up against it were black plastic trash bags in a row, a few grocery carts filled with more plastic bags, a cardboard sign on which someone had written *I used to be your neighbor*, and another one, on which *ANYTHING HELPS* had been printed in large black capitals in the middle of a circle of sloppy-looking happy faces, and in the midst of it all, a seriously overweight golden retriever with matted yellow hair, curled up, asleep. She assumed no one was trapped between her car and the curb because the people who were gathering around her car—closing in on her like zombies really—were looking at *her*. No one was looking down where a pinned body might have been.

Her second conscious thought was for the driver of the car that had struck her, the car that had pushed her off course. She glanced to her right to look out her passenger window, most of the glass of which was in fragments on the passenger seat. The car that had hit her was old, dirty, grayish brown, maybe an early model Ford Taurus, if she had to guess. The driver—it was a man, a dazed-looking man, she could see that much even through his filthy windshield and the steam rising up from under his now protracted hood— had to have been going mighty fast, and right through the stop sign, to have broadsided her like this.

Someone opened her door, and immediately her nose filled with the smells of burnt rubber, oil, gas, chemicals, while her ears filled with voices, male and female, the people who had been on the curb, all yelling at once over the persistent hissing coming from under her hood. "Are you all right? Are you all right?" everyone was asking. "I'll run in and call for help," a man shouted. Someone else said, "Her airbag didn't deploy. Why didn't her airbag deploy?" Someone answered, "It don't always happen like that. She wasn't going fast enough." "Yeah, but—" the previous speaker said, "shoulda. Shoulda deployed." Some of the people had gone to the other car, the Taurus, and a few were screaming at the driver. "What the fuck is wrong with you?" a man shouted. "Didn't you see the fucking stop sign?"

Suddenly there were hands on Lola. They seemed to be everywhere at once. She looked up into the faces that went with them. They were black, white, Hispanic, Native, and Asian, their ages ranging too: a virtual poster for diversity. She saw black holes where teeth belonged, cheeks streaked with dirt and drawn with hunger, smudged eyeglasses held together with strips of red duct tape, sweat-stained baseball caps, hair straggly and greasy. She smelled cigarette smoke and body odor. She began to swat at the hands, some of which seemed to be moving across her chest. She continued swatting even when it sunk in that they were only trying to undo her seatbelt, ease her out of her seat.

Now she heard a new sound. It took a few beats for her to realize it was her, moaning. She thought she must be badly injured, dying perhaps. It's true she'd been unhappy, and for quite a long time now. But she knew what happiness looked like, and she wanted more years, more life, a chance, if not to attain happiness, then at least to make improvements in that direction. She wanted to go out on a high note, so that if she *did* have to come back, she wouldn't find herself grappling with the same obstacles, the consequence of lessons gone unlearned.

She imagined she had parts missing, that which ones they were would become obvious once the shock wore off. Her heart was beating rapidly, but she couldn't find the strength to lift her hand to it. "Let's try and get you out of the car," a female voice said. Another voice, a man's, said, "You're not supposed to move them." "Oh, yeah, Asswipe," said the female, her tone gone shrill. "You smell gas, Asswipe? You don't leave the vic in the car when it's about to blow." Asswipe didn't respond.

Lola allowed herself to be lifted. Simultaneously, she watched her bag, also being lifted, by a young man wearing the kind of shirt Lola knew was called a wifebeater. She wondered if that was Asswipe, if Asswipe intended to steal her purse. *Don't judge, don't judge*, she told herself. It was her mantra of late, devised to deal with what she believed to be her greatest character flaw. She forced herself to look away from Asswipe, to trust that he would hold onto her bag until the ambulance came, that he wouldn't fumble inside for her wallet.

Every bit of her was shaking; she was shaking from the inside out. All her organs were vibrating; she could feel them. She was dragged up onto the sidewalk, supported by two strong women, one holding each arm, and she was glad for that because she didn't think she could have stood on her own. She dared to look down, and she was relieved to see that both her legs were still there, both feet attached.

The man who hit her was out of his car too now. He had gotten his mojo back, apparently, and he was screaming at the people who had surrounded him, and they were screaming back. When he shoved one man out of his way, his face came into view, and Lola shuddered to find him looking right at her, scowling, like the accident had been *her* fault. He appeared to be Hispanic—short but solid, maybe in his mid-forties. His face and neck were covered with tattoos, ornate Roman numerals on his forehead, a teardrop to the side of one eye—she knew what that meant, that he had killed someone—and what looked like random designs on his neck. *Don't judge*, she told herself. *Don't judge, don't judge, don't judge.* "Yeah, take a good look," one of the women who was holding her yelled. "You see what you did, dumb fuck, motherfucker? You coulda killed this nice woman."

The sound of a siren, at last, recognizable even over all the yelling and screaming going on. The perp heard it too. He stiffened, and then all at once he bolted. The people in the crowd that had been surrounding him began yelling at the top of their lungs. *Scumbag. Asshole. Fucking gang-banger. Coward. Run, you coward, run.* A police car came around the corner so fast its tires screeched. The crowd hollered and pointed to the perp, halfway down the street already, about to run into someone's yard. The police car went screaming after him. Then the car stopped and two officers jumped out, leaving the car doors wide open behind them. With their weapons drawn, they ran into the yard where the perp had disappeared.

Except for the hissing sounds both cars were making, there was silence then. The crowd seemed to be holding its collective breath as it waited to see what would happen next. All at once there was a popping sound, which Lola would not have recognized as a gunshot if someone near her had not mumbled, "Fucker deserved that."

Lola looked at the faces around her in wonder. Could all this really be happening? Only moments ago she had been driving slowly down Second Avenue, thinking about the house she'd just come from. She'd met with the family there for the first time two weeks earlier, a husband and wife and a teenage son, and the wife's mother, who had Alzheimer's. The dog was for her, the old lady, Mary. Lola had brought three dogs along that first visit, a spaniel mix, a border collie mix, and a pug, and Mary went wild for Susie Q, the pug, a well-mannered five-year-old that Lola had trained herself. The family seemed fine, so Lola had agreed to present her board of directors with the paperwork—a formality really—recommending that Susie Q become Mary's companion. But when she went today to drop off the dog, there was a situation going on. The wife, who opened the door a good three minutes after Lola's third ring of the bell, had puffy red eyes, and upon seeing Lola standing there, the son, who had come up behind his mother, glowered, turned, and ran upstairs and slammed a door. Only the father, who came to the door next, seemed the same. But whereas he had given Lola a good impression during her first visit, this time his cheerful demeanor seemed blatantly contrived. Nobody invited her in. The wife, her arms folded around herself, backed away from the door, and the husband took Susie Q's leash and records folder from Lola out on the stoop. He smiled a thank you and shut the door in her face.

And that was that. It made Lola sick inside to see that that man was able to grin like that when his wife had been crying and his son was acting out. And where was the old lady? Lola had looked forward to meeting with her again, just to ensure that her enthusiasm for Susie Q was still evident. Alzheimer's patients could be unpredictable in their preferences.

As soon as she got in her car and pulled out of the driveway she regretted leaving Susie Q behind. That's what she had been thinking about, that, and, more abstractedly, that the people on the curb she was passing were a motley crew—and then *bang!* Everything changed. And now here she was, standing, by the grace of the two strong but rather stinky strangers holding her up, out on the curb, her car cratered, and the police down the street pursuing the man who had hit her.

Everyone was still focused on the cop car, waiting for the cops and the perp to come back into view. Lola felt calmer; the quaking of her organs had abated, but now she thought she felt too calm, like maybe some of her parts were in the process of shutting down. She was three years short of sixty, after all. How much would it take for some essential organs to quit on her? She glanced to the side, beyond the curb where the people had been sitting just before she'd almost killed them all. She looked at the building, the sign over the door, one of the city's homeless shelters. Of course. She should have realized. She would have if she'd been thinking clearly.

There were even more people gathered around her now than there had been at first. Apparently people who had been inside the shelter had come out to see what was happening. Some of them were not homeless; some of them worked at the shelter. You could tell because some were nicely dressed, with shiny hair and bright eyes and perky expressions and bodies that looked well fed, a few of them a little too much so.

Lola was taking it all in when she happened to see something suspicious, a man moving stealthily just beyond the crowd—tall, with a salt-and-pepper beard and longish wavy dark hair sticking out the back of his baseball cap— wearing a bulky asparagus-green baseball jacket with an embroidered P patch sewn over the front pocket. This was Albuquerque in the summer, probably close to one hundred degrees in the shade on this particular day. And it wasn't only that: the man had something *under* his jacket. He was supporting its weight with both arms, trying to look like he wasn't, trying to look like he had a stomachache, maybe. He glanced at the crowd, furtively, she thought, and pulled open the door to the shelter. Just before he entered, he looked back once more and his eye fell on Lola and their gazes locked. It was only a split second, but in that instant she saw his face freeze and she knew for certain that he was up to no good and that he knew that she knew that. Lola turned to the woman on her right, whose grip was still tight on her arm. "That man," she whimpered. The woman, who had a dirty blue bandana tied around her head, patted Lola's arm with her free hand. "Don't you worry, sweetie," she said. "The Five-0s are handling it."

"But, but," she tried again. She had to let someone know that something bad was happening, that someone had used this unfolding drama as an excuse to sneak into the building with a gun—or a bomb! "But, but," she went on, but then there was another siren, getting louder every second, drowning out not only her plea but also her apprehension concerning the man in the asparagus jacket.

The ambulance turned the corner and the siren stopped shrieking abruptly. *Finally*, Lola thought, *finally*. She glanced down the street. One of the police officers was standing near the car, talking on his cell phone. The perp and the other officer had still not reappeared. The woman beside her said, to no one in particular, "That was quick." *Quick?* Lola wondered. *Really? This*, she thought, *is what it feels like when time stands still.*

But everything did happen fast thereafter. The EMTs, two men in their twenties, one thin and reedy and the other short and muscular, jumped out as fast as the police had jumped out of their vehicle and marched right up to Lola and started asking her questions. She found her tongue, her voice. She told them her name, the date, the name of the current president and then the name of the previous one (though she had promised herself she would never say that one's name out loud again, unless she used it as a verb), the month of the year, everything they wanted to know. They asked her what happened, and she would have told them that too, but it was the question everyone had been waiting for, apparently; the entire crowd pressed forward, all of them talking at once, offering slightly different versions of the same story. Meanwhile, the thin EMT touched Lola's neck. "That hurt?"

"A little."

He placed the flat of his hand on her upper back. "What about that?"

"A little. Everything hurts a little."

"Can you move your legs for me? Let me see you move your legs."

Lola kicked one leg out straight, then the other. She chuckled a little. She looked up from her feet to see a second ambulance rounding the corner, this one sans siren. It blasted past the accident scene and zoomed down the road and came to a screeching halt just behind the police car.

"Ma'am," the thin EMT said, "please." He had removed a gurney from the vehicle and was pointing down at it. The women who had been supporting Lola held on to her as she bent to sit on the gurney. The EMT had to physically detach their fingers so that he could guide Lola into a horizontal position. In a few seconds flat, she was strapped in and being slid into the back of the ambulance. As he secured the gurney, the muscular EMT explained that she looked to be perfectly fine, but it made good sense for her to get checked out over at the hospital, just in case.

Lola lifted her head to take one last look at the people who had gathered around her on this momentous occasion. She found herself full of love for each and every one of them. They had stood by her, on this day of days that she would never forget; they had been witnesses to this small fragment of her life, which was nothing if not a microcosm of the greater whole. Some of them stared back at her, their expressions equally loving, or at least pensive; others scrutinized the equipment inside the back of the ambulance: monitors, medical kits, splints, an oxygen tank. The EMTs shooed them back so they could jump down.

They were about to shut the double doors when a man's voice yelled, "Wait, wait, don't forget her bag." The thin EMT took it from him and tossed it on the floor near Lola's head. Lola could tell just by the *thunk* it made that it was as heavy as it had ever been, that her wallet, which was always loaded with loose change—because she was one of those few people who preferred to pay in cash when she had the option—remained intact. Holding her head up as high as she could with the gurney straps cutting into her chest and arms, she took a deep breath, so as to be able to project her voice, and just before the doors finally did close she managed to say, "Thank you, Asswipe. Thank you for everything."

2

BEN

entanglement

Dolly, one of the full-timers, came out from the kitchen carrying the Yankees cap that she used for the daily drawing and cleared her throat. "Everyone, quiet down and listen up," she shouted.

The diners barely glanced at her. She said the same exact thing every day, and the truth was, it was an unnecessary directive, because hardly anyone who could make it to the shelter this early in the morning was interested in talking anyway. If there was any chat going on, it was coming from the volunteer servers, who were forever trying to engage the down-and-outers, as Ben thought of the community he was now a part of, with their cheerful witticisms.

"Okay, is everyone ready?" Dolly shrieked. She dipped her fingers into the Yankees cap and tittered as she pulled forth the first number.

Ben regarded her with mild disgust. Her immoderate smile confirmed that this drawing was one of the highlights of her day. Dolly, who was not much older than his own daughter, had nice features, a pretty face. It was a shame she was about one hundred pounds overweight. It was a shame someone—her mother or a close friend—hadn't bothered to

11

sit her down and explain that her whole life would change if she would just make some lifestyle adjustments. Ben was obsessed these days with the small things that could bring about change—good *or* bad—into a life. A left turn instead of a right, a message deleted before it was listened to …

"Okay," shouted Dolly, "now listen for your number. If you miss out because you don't hear me, you leave me no choice but to pick someone else."

That smile again, and then how she took her time announcing the numbers, savoring the attention—if you could call it that—focused on her. Heartbreaking, Ben thought, a young woman with her whole future ahead of her. He was so busy thinking about Dolly, and behind that, thinking about Moon, his daughter, that he almost missed it when she screamed, "Twenty-six."

That was him! He was number twenty-six! The number was right there, in black marker on the corner of his dull red plastic tray. But he was still holding his tray (on which sat toast, some kind of mush that might have been oatmeal the previous day, two strips of bacon, a container of milk, and a cup of coffee), and he couldn't lift his arm the way he would have liked, so instead he shouted, "Damn!" Dolly had called twenty-six and he was twenty-six and that meant that tonight he would get to sleep in a bed, on a cot in a room that was air-conditioned.

Once in a blue moon, right? He realized he was smiling, wildly by the feel of it. He was looking at Dolly and she was looking back at him and they were both smiling the same way. "Damn!" he said again. He saw tears glistening in her blue-gray eyes. He thought there might be some in his too. In that instant some vague barrier between them dissipated and something new formed in its place.

Already he was imagining it: the crisp white sheets, the scent of detergent, a tinge of bleach. A down pillow beneath his head. Or any pillow, didn't have to be down. But of course he had some obstacles to overcome before he could lay himself down and savor the promise of a good night's sleep.

He ate all the mush and toast and one strip of bacon with his coffee, pocketed the container of milk and the other piece of bacon, and hurried out and around the corner of the building to where Nancy was leaning up against the brick with Siggy, his big gray cat, at her feet. "He was good," she said as he approached. He had to smile. Siggy was in his canvas pet carrier, which didn't really allow much opportunity for being bad. And besides that, Siggy was eighteen years old. The prospect of causing a ruckus didn't excite him the way it used to.

"Thank you for watching him, Nance," Ben said, and he bent forward to kiss her on her head. She was short; she had to tip her head back to smile up at him. Her eyes were big and very blue, deep pools of flat-out hardship.

He'd spent a night with Nancy the week before. She'd come out to the overpass with him and they'd settled side by side on his sleeping bag out on the ledge beneath it and talked for three or four hours, until they both fell asleep. She'd told him her story, how she'd wound up on the street. She'd suspected her husband was doing drugs, but she didn't know it was smack, and she didn't know he was sleeping with his pusher. He'd loved Nancy, that she *did* know. Sure, their relationship had been rocky at times, but they had loved each other madly from day one. But all the pressure—from the pusher, she supposed, from having to keep up appearances at work (he was a graphic designer, freelancing for a couple of local magazines), from having to lie to Nancy to cover up for his demons—must have become too much for him because he swamped. Nancy came home from the grocery store one afternoon and found him out in the garage, where he'd used a yellow extension cord to hang himself from a rafter. Thinking maybe he was still alive, hoping against all hope that he was still alive, Nancy found a ladder and worked him loose. Little did she know that she would relive those moments— her rocketing panic, the feel of his dead weight slamming against her as the cord came free—night and day, awake or dreaming, ever after.

She only learned about the pusher later, she'd told Ben that night out on the ledge—whispering because Ben's space mates were there too, though both were snoring by then— after the ambulance had come and gone, when she'd listened to the voicemails her husband had never bothered to delete from his cell phone. The pusher was needy; that was clear. She was keeping him coming for the transaction, yeah, but she was wanting so much more from him too. Her voice on the phone sounded like a lifetime of bad karma and cigarettes. Nancy figured he'd left the messages purposely, so she'd listen and understand how it was, how breaking with the pusher would be breaking with the drug, and how he didn't have the muscle for it. What she couldn't figure out was why he hadn't let her hear the messages earlier, when he was still alive. That was the question that went around and around in her head, driving her crazy. She would have understood, she said. Together they could have worked out a solution.

She called the woman that night, to let her know Phil was dead and to demand the details of their relationship. In her moment of grief, the woman, whose name was Estelle, gave her everything she wanted and more. Too much, in fact.

Nancy thought it would help to see the whole picture, but she never got back on her feet again after that. Phil and Estelle had had a full relationship. He'd met her kids and, once, even her mother. They'd gone places together, like a family. They'd attended her best friend's daughter's high school graduation together. He'd spilled grape juice on his shirt that night, at the afterparty. Did Nancy remember him coming home with a cloud of purple over his heart? They'd laughed about it: his first purple heart. (Nancy hadn't noticed at the time, but she told Ben it was now a stain she would never forget.) It was like learning that Phil time-traveled to a different planet whenever she turned her back. Estelle insisted he never mentioned her when they were together. She was vapor, suspended in the distance, a blur of haze in a corner where no one would ever think to look. Worse than invisible.

This was the power of addiction, Nancy said. This was how far Phil had had to bend for the sake of the drug. She didn't believe for a moment that he loved that woman. It wasn't possible. But her conversation with Estelle stayed with her, distracted her to the point where she had to quit her job (working as a secretary for the local Chamber of Commerce) because she couldn't concentrate. They'd never owned anything outright, she and Phil, except their vehicles. They'd had no savings. For a while she lived on the money she made selling his truck and a few other items, and when that ran out she moved out of the small rental they'd shared and started sleeping in her car. The $500 a month she got from Phil's insurance death benefit—it would have been twice that if not for the fact that he was a suicide—was enough to keep her old Jetta running, to pay Mrs. Quick, the old woman who allowed her to park in her driveway at night and to use the small bathroom located in the shed behind her house, to pay the shrink she saw once a week for her PTSD, and to take care of a few personal needs, including a meal or two when she couldn't get to the shelter—but no more.

"Hey, guess what," Ben said.

Nancy turned her blues on him again.

"They picked my number. I'm sleeping here tonight."

Her mouth went from heart-shaped to oval. "Oh, good for you, Ben!" She went up on her toes, her hands pressed together like someone offering a *namaste* at the end of a yoga class. "I never bother to sign up, because I've got the Jetta. Maybe in winter. Would seem unfair this time of year."

Her mention of fairness reminded him that the kitchen would be closing soon. "You better hurry in," he said, "before they run out of food."

Nancy lifted her brows in agreement, flashed a pretty smile, and turned and hurried toward the front of the building. As he watched her go, he admitted to himself that there was a mutual attraction there, and he'd just bet she'd feel really good to hold in his arms, but he couldn't imagine having a serious relationship with a fellow down-and-outer because, well, because he planned to reverse his circumstances quickly, and he didn't want the responsibility of someone else's circumstances, not at this time at least. Maybe later when he was back on his feet. He'd noticed over the last few weeks that the down-and-outers who formed relationships with one another—at least the older ones, in their forties or fifties or sixties—were mostly those who had lost all hope, who expected this to be forever. Who believed this was as good as it would ever get.

Unless you had someone watching your stuff, you had to drag it around with you, because there were a lot of down-and-outers who didn't have much stuff of their own, and everyone knew to put survival over the dictates of conscience. Ben's stuff was usually not a concern, because he and his space mates, the two men he shared the overpass ledge with, took turns keeping an eye on one another's things. But as it happened, both Derrick and Vince were leaving the ledge that night to attend an illegal horse race on someone's ranch out in the South Valley. So, after he broke up the bacon and fed it to Siggy and poured some of the milk from the carton into the plastic dish he kept in the carrier's side pocket, Ben made his way back to the overpass, about a mile and a half west of the shelter, to retrieve his belongings.

Derrick wasn't there when he arrived, only Vince. He gave Vince what was left of the milk and told him about his number being called. "I don't know, man," Vince said after draining the carton. "You mess up your rhythm trying to fit yourself into the white man's world."

Ben laughed. "I *am* white. So are you, mostly. What are you talking about?"

"Yeah, but …" Vince drifted off; he lifted the index finger of his right hand and stared at it. Ben could see it was red and swollen. "Yeah, but we don't *live* in the white man's world no more. We be blue or orange or green by now, even though we still *look* whiteish, mostly."

"Well, I'm going for it, and I'll let you know how it was when I see you again tomorrow. Meantime I got to drag all my stuff over there."

They both looked at Ben's stuff—his sleeping bag, which he'd rolled up earlier; a double trash bag full of his extra clothing and personal effects; a backpack he'd bought for his daughter years ago, which she'd never used because she hated the color (mud brown, she'd called it); and, of course, the black canvas cat carrier. "How you gonna carry everything?" Vince asked.

"I'll manage."

Vince looked at the pet carrier. "Why don't you leave the kitty cat with me while you take your other stuff over, and then come back and get him. I got no plans until my cousin comes to pick up me and Derrick tonight."

Ben thought about that. In the four weeks that he'd been living on the ledge (he'd spent some time living in a friend's shed prior to that) he hadn't left Siggy with anyone, except for the few minutes it took to swallow down a meal at the shelter. And even then, he wouldn't leave him unless it was someone like Nancy, or one of the other nice women he'd come to know, standing right outside. There was one time he walked all the way to the shelter and then never even ate, because he didn't see anyone standing around that he felt comfortable leaving Siggy with for even a few minutes.

Eighteen years he'd had Siggy Hopper Frey, since he was a little kitten. He'd named him Sigurth, after the legendary dragon slayer from Norse mythology, and Moon had given him the middle name, Hopper (she was ten then), because of Siggy's inclination to arch his back and propel himself straight up, high into the air. You'd come down the stairs early in the morning, groggy with sleep, and, bam! Siggy would hop out right in front you, out of nowhere, out of thin air, like he'd been waiting all night long for the chance to scare the bejeezus out of you. He did the same thing when you walked in the door in the late afternoon, bouncing two, three feet high, like he had magic springs in his little legs.

But even then he'd had this other side too, cuddling up on your chest, purring so loud that Ruthie would swear she could hear him from the next room, exuding so much profound tranquility that eventually it soaked into you as well. When you talked to Siggy, he looked right at you, no matter how long you rambled on. Ben was convinced he knew what you were saying, or at least he knew what Ben was saying. Siggy knew more of Ben's secrets than anyone else in the world.

"Come on, man," urged Vince, disgusted. "I can see your wheels turning, man. Turning and turning and turning." He made three slow rotations with the swollen finger. "They turn enough, man, they're gonna fall the fuck off! You know that? What the fuck you think I'm going to do, eat him?"

Eat him? Ben had to look away. He was horrified to think that Vince would even say something like that, even if it *was* supposed to be a joke. Vince was a young guy, maybe in his early thirties, a smart ass. Why he was homeless Ben had no idea. He'd never said and Ben had never asked him. His body posture alone—always sitting on the edge of the ledge, his gaze unwavering but focused on nothing— signaled that he wasn't one for confidence sharing. Derrick, the other man who shared the ledge, was slow, probably retarded, or developmentally disabled, as Ruthie always reminded him was the right way to say it. Ben asked about him once and one of the women at the shelter said he just plain ran out of family. He'd lived with his parents—watching TV and munching potato chips all day—until he was well into his forties, and when his parents died, within a couple of years of each other, his younger sister and her husband took him in. But then his sister died too, in an auto accident, and the husband didn't want him, and the only other sibling was recently divorced, and what was she going to do with him? So now he was out on the street. He was on a waiting list for a group home, but everyone knew that was a joke. You could wait for years, social services being what they were, and by that time a person like Derrick was likely to have forgotten the manners, the behaviors you needed to exhibit to make the cut. Ben worried about him, because he was the type to walk into trouble without even realizing it.

Vince was glaring at him, waiting for an answer. Derrick liked Siggy a lot. Ben would have felt better if he were around, but he wasn't. So Ben caved and said, "Thanks, Vince. I owe you a solid. I'll be quick." He wanted to add, *But please, please, please, don't let anything happen to my cat—* though of course he didn't.

Ben gathered his sleeping bag and his trash bag and backpack and headed back to the shelter. It was getting warm by then, and it wasn't an easy walk anyway as he had to cross the interstate and then cut through some fields that were home to rock squirrels. Not only were rock squirrels homely as fuck—looking more like rats than any squirrels Ben had ever seen back in Connecticut, where he'd lived the first many years of his life—but they dug burrows, which were easy to trip on when you were moving along at a good clip, carrying stuff in both arms. And worse, they were known carriers of plague.

Ben got to the shelter just after it reopened for early lunch. He was still worrying about Siggy, but he was hungry too, and it was extremely rare to see Salisbury steak with gravy and mashed potatoes on the lunch menu. Usually it was sandwiches, and never enough to go around. And today the line wasn't that long, probably because it was supposed to hit a hundred degrees within the next few hours.

Before eating he checked in with Dolly, who unlocked the door to the men's dorm, and since he was the first one to show up, told him to pick whatever cot he wanted for the night. There were some twenty cots in a room that was maybe twenty feet across and forty feet long. He chose the cot in the innermost corner, where he thought he would most easily be able to conceal Siggy. He dropped his sleeping bag on the cot and then pulled the cot away from the wall and stashed his trash bag and backpack in the space he'd created. The carrier would have to go there too, because there wasn't enough space under the cot.

Ben glanced over his shoulder. Dolly was watching from the doorway, one hand on her hip and the other on the doorknob, waiting for him to hurry along so she could lock up behind him. He reached his hand into his trash bag and retrieved his jacket and rolled it up and stuck it under his arm like a football. Then he hurried out, thanking Dolly as he passed her. He got on the food line, received his tray and wolfed down his lunch, saving some of the meat scraps in a napkin for Siggy.

Maybe because he no longer had the burden of his possessions to juggle, his obstinate mind went into panic mode as soon as he was back outdoors. He kept hearing that crack Vince had made about eating Siggy, the sarcasm in his voice. What did he know about Vince anyway except that he had a mean streak? Once, when the three of them were sitting on the edge the ledge, waiting for time to slither by, Vince threw a small rock down on the bike path below just as a biker was peddling by. The biker, a middle-aged woman, yelped and then glanced up and saw them sitting up there, watching her like three monkeys on a limb. Her face went white with terror. Her bike wobbled, and she could have fallen easily enough. Vince laughed. Derrick laughed too, because he was good-natured and he thought that was what you were supposed to do when someone else laughed first. Ben said, "The fuck?" and Vince replied, "It was only a pebble, man, and it didn't even hit her. If I meant to hit her I would of." "Pebble or not," Ben responded, "she wobbled; she could have fallen." "Yeah, so," Vince said, "she would have hit the guardrail. That's what it's there for."

It was true there was a guardrail at the outside edge of the bike path, and below it a sharply sloped concrete wall leading to the deep arroyo at the bottom. But she still could have broken her neck, depending on how she fell. Ben climbed down to have a look a little later. It wasn't a pebble; it was definitely a rock. He threw it into the arroyo and shook his head at the shit-fest his life had become.

He walked faster, ducking under eaves as he made his way through town, because now it was really hot. He kept his head tipped down. He didn't want to run into anyone he knew. His intention always was to spare old friends and ac-quaintances alike the embarrassment of having to decide whether or not to acknowledge him.

When he hit the fields he began to jog. Siggy was all he had in the world. Ruthie had been reluctant to give him up, but she had the dogs, two beautiful Goldens, and Fry—Fry Frey, the younger cat, named in happier times—and of course Moon, who still lived at home even though she was coming up on twenty-eight. Thanks to Ben, Ruthie's savings were somewhat reduced, but she still had the house. She still had her job. And she had her car. The ends met, more or less.

She didn't need Siggy to make her life be all right, and he did. His argument had been that Siggy didn't have much longer anyway. Did she *really* want to deal with an eighteen-year-old cat? If he got sick on her watch, she knew damn well she'd feel obligated to spend money she didn't have taking him to the vet, taking time off from work (she was an assistant for an acupuncturist; if she didn't come in, her boss had to run back and forth between the back rooms where the patients were and the front desk and waiting room; she didn't like it, and Ruthie couldn't afford to be fired), whereas if Siggy got sick while in Ben's care, there was nothing he could do about it. He remembered the look Ruthie had given him when he said that. Like he'd called her number and she knew it. And still she said no. No, he couldn't take the cat. He took him anyway.

Vince had gone through his bag once; there was that too. Ben knew because things that had been at the bottom had shifted to the sides. Nothing was gone, but that wasn't the point. It couldn't have been Derrick. Derrick wouldn't do a thing like that—unless Vince made him, and then Derrick would have slipped and said something about it.

Ben began to run. He had a bad feeling that he had made a terrible mistake leaving Siggy behind. His recent life was a series of mistakes, a pileup—twenty cars worth, maybe fifty. He could feel the sweat running down his forehead, stinging his eyeballs, sticking to his neck.

There was something sleazy about Vince, like him dragging Derrick to illegal events like the one they were going to tonight. Bad things happened at illegal horse races. There was a lot at stake for the lowlife ranch owners who hosted them. They wanted everyone falling-down drunk, making huge bets to cover their risks. And the horses, most of them were pumped up with drugs, improperly trained, and being ridden by wannabe jockeys for whom the use of electric shock devices was only the tip of the "prodding" iceberg. There were guns around too, in case things got out of hand. If something happened, it could easily be covered up. You could attend an event like that and never be seen or heard from again.

Vince was small but fit; Vince was streetwise. He could take care of himself. Derrick was something of a dumb giant. The spare tire around his waist was big enough to accommodate a small car, a Ford Fiesta maybe. He was clumsy; he tripped over his own feet. Ben held his breath whenever Derrick climbed up from the ledge to the interstate, for fear he would lose his footing and slip back down the embankment and crack his head. His most prized possession was a green plastic owl Vince had found in someone's trash. He'd taken it because he thought it might help keep the pigeons away. It didn't, really; pigeons are smarter than that. But Derrick had come to care for the thing, and he begged Vince to let him keep it. Vince would have gotten rid of it on spite, just to demean him, but Ben got involved. He said he for one felt safer having a deterrent up there, even if it only scared away one or two pigeons a day. Who was to say the one pigeon it frightened off wasn't the one that was disease-carrying? Both men knew that wasn't what the argument was about. But, surprisingly, Vince backed down anyway. As for Derrick, when he thought Vince wasn't paying attention he whispered to the thing, just a word or two, a greeting or a reassurance. He patted its head with his chubby fingers. He smoothed the ridges meant to indicate feathers. He was forever inching it closer to his side. Ben had no doubt that if Vince and Derrick encountered danger, whether at the horse race or elsewhere, Vince would fade back—or worse, fade out —and let Derrick take the heat.

There were people out in the field near the overpass. Ben wasn't close enough to see who they were, but when anyone was out there it was a concern. There'd been two murders in the area in recent years. In both instances thugs had pulled over on the shoulder of the interstate, dragged their victims over the guard rail and out onto the field (which dipped down from the freeway, offering concealment), killed them, and then rolled the bodies down the embankment so that they bounced past the ledge and wound up on the bike trail for innocent peddlers to discover in the morning. There'd been other criminal activities out there too—drug deals and beatings, and once a rape. The location made it easy for the thugs to hop back into their cars and get away clean. When he'd first considered asking Vince if he could stay on the ledge, Ben had had to weigh the prospect of yet another atrocity with the fact that the ledge provided relative privacy and shelter from the weather. Vince, who'd been living on the ledge for months by the time Ben came along—and who was not opposed to having someone besides Derrick to watch his stuff when he had to be away—had put forth the final argument. "Long as you keep your mouth shut and don't climb up to investigate, they ain't even gonna know you're here," he'd said, referring to the evildoers.

Ben was getting close now and he could see it wasn't thugs after all; it was someone cooking something in a fry pan over one of those mini spirit burners. There was a sudden buildup of pressure in his brain when he realized that that someone was Vince. Derrick was with him, sitting on the ground, watching, his knees pulled up, his arms halfway around them, rocking himself back and forth. Within seconds Ben was almost blind from the blood surging to his head. How could he have forgotten about the spirit burner? Now and then Vince would send Derrick out to steal fuel for it from one of the sporting goods stores up on the highway. Mostly Derrick came back empty-handed, but when he scored, Vince would kill something, anything, a rock squirrel or a pigeon, and they'd cook it out in the field—Vince's idea of a picnic.

Ben began to run faster, but he was running drunk now, drunk on dread, stumbling along like someone whose feet had gone numb. Terror had sucked away his coordination. He could hardly hold himself upright. He was going to kill Vince. He was going to choke him to death. He didn't care if it meant going back to jail. His life was over anyway, living on a ledge under an overpass, where you had to walk bent in half so as not to bang your head, with these two losers, with rats, with roaches and spiders, the endless rumble of trucks, the whiz of cars, right above your head, day and night. Jail had been easier and less degrading. He could already feel Vince's skinny neck under his fingers.

He couldn't see. He was running blind, the blood in his head and the sweat and tears in his eyes ... The carrier was there all right, right at Vince's side, and he was going to kill him. Vince knew it too now. As Ben got closer, Vince's smile retreated and his eyes began to bulge. He was about to die and he knew it. Good. He was in a squat position over the burner, but he was backing away, getting ready to shoot up to his full size, which Ben was glad for, because he wanted to pummel him good before he killed him. He'd never wanted anything so badly in his life. He was already pulling every-thing he had—every heartbreak, every broken promise, every bad decision, every violation—into his fist, and he couldn't wait to smash it into the middle of Vince's head. He couldn't wait to turn Vince's ugly face into soup. Didn't matter that Vince was probably close to thirty years younger than him. Ben had fury on his side.

Just as he was about to pounce he saw a movement from the corner of his eye. Siggy. *Derrick* had Siggy cradled in the space between his legs and his balloon gut; Siggy on his back, as content as a newborn baby, twisting his head around to look at Ben. *What the fuck?* he seemed to be asking. *What the fuck, Dad?* Ben looked at the fry pan balanced on the tiny burner. The thing in it was small. "Squab," Vince mumbled with disgust.

Ben collapsed on the ground and covered his head with one arm and began to sob. In rushed Moon, putting on her makeup behind the half-open bathroom door, her dress too tight on top, too short at bottom. She was so smart. All good grades growing up, a degree in English Lit from the local university. She'd loved poetry. She'd read it to him; she'd explained everything she learned in her lit classes and he'd listened carefully—because he really wanted to understand how she navigated through her world, how she explored it, what she saw. He had loved poetry once too, long ago, but then he'd gone a different way. Listening to her talk about Whitman's transcendentalism or Ted Hughes' cynicism, he was willing to be led back again.

She'd planned to teach, his Moon; the job at Starbucks was only something to do until she finished her masters. But then she stalled. She didn't want to teach anymore. All she wanted, as far as he had been able to tell, was to meet someone. But who would ever find her under all that makeup? Inside that flimsy dress? And when he'd said that—not that exactly but that maybe she should tone it down, meaning, in that particular instant, the black paint or whatever it was on her eyelids, the matching lipstick—she told him to fuck himself, that after what he'd done to her and Ruthie he had no right to criticize anybody ever again. She'd said other things previously: "people in glass houses" and "look who's calling the kettle." But she'd never told him to fuck himself until then.

Time passed. Eventually Ben stopped sobbing and got down to deep breaths that left him spuming on the exhale. Then, at last, he quieted altogether.

Gradually the hum of the traffic on the interstate returned, along with the feel of the hot sun on his back, the lump that was his rolled-up jacket, still tucked under one arm. Moon's face, ugly with warpaint and hatred, began to fade, and he realized that the sandy earth beneath his face was wet with tears and snot and saliva and sweat. Vince said, softly, seriously, drawing out each word, "You are one hell of an asshole, man." The words fell into a pit of silence. Then Derrick said, "Go to Daddy, Siggy." And Siggy did. Derrick put him down on the ground and he strolled over and draped himself on the back of Ben's sweat-soaked neck and immediately began to purr. Ben reached back to touch him. His fingers found Siggy's collar. Derrick had attached his leash, just as Ben was always instructing him. It was taut; Derrick was still holding the other end of it, as a precaution, in case Siggy tried to run away. Ben began to cry all over again.

Later, after Derrick and Vince had finished eating the pigeon and joined Ben out on the ledge, Ben offered to have a look at Vince's finger. He figured Vince would tell him to fuck off, and he deserved that, but Vince surprised him and scooted over to show it to him. "Light, Derrick," Vince snapped—because it was dark on the ledge at all times of day—and Derrick got his flashlight out of his trash bag, and after a quick pat to Owl's head, scooted over to sit on Ben's other side.

It was a splinter, a really thick one. The finger was infected. Ben's fingers were dirty, and he didn't have a needle or a saucer of hot water and baking soda or antibacterial cream or even a Band-Aid. All he had was Derrick with the flashlight.

Vince howled when Ben began to knead the flesh surrounding the spot where the splinter had entered, but he didn't pull away. Instead he turned his head aside and began to pant, the way women do when they're having labor pains. He was so good at it that Ben thought he must have been to Lamaze classes at some point in his life, which would indicate that he'd had a woman once, and, unless something went terribly wrong, she'd had a baby. This was the wrong time to ask him about it, though. "Bring the light closer, Derrick," he mumbled.

Derrick got closer with the light. He was humming low and tunelessly, something he did when he was nervous or scared. Vince's controlled breathing got louder, now punctuated with whimpers of pain. "Come on," Ben coaxed the splinter. "Come on out, baby."

He continued to work the flesh of Vince's finger, trying to gauge the angle the splinter had gone in at. Moon wouldn't let Ruthie near her when she had a splinter, only Ben, because, she'd always said, "Daddy doesn't hurt." *Daddy hurts all right*, he thought to himself. *Daddy hurts real bad.* He'd cried like a baby earlier, Siggy riding his heaving shoulders like a regular cowpoke. And Vince hadn't said a word. Neither had Derrick. Derrick hadn't even hummed. They had to have known they were witnessing a man hitting rock bottom, a man so close to hell on Earth that he could emulate its sounds, its posture. He was *hell* in that moment. Hell personified.

The head of the splinter emerged, a couple of millimeters, no more. Derrick was still humming. He moved closer to see, and before Ben knew it, his head was leaning against Ben's shoulder. That was fine, even though he stunk—they all did—as long as he kept the light steady, which he did. Vince was still looking in the opposite direction, breathing, maybe crying a little too now. Ben lifted Vince's dirty finger—a finger that had skinned a dead pigeon today, and probably worse—to his mouth; it had to be done. He found the head of the splinter with his front teeth. He tried not to think about the dirt, the germs. This was this and cleanliness was a time and place that existed only in his memory. Nor did he let himself dwell on the fact that he didn't even really like Vince. As long as they lived under the same overpass together, the three of them constituted an unconventional family, bound not by love and not by blood but by space and circumstance, by the indifference of everyone they had known in their respective pasts, by their mistakes, or, in Derrick's case, by circumstances beyond anyone's control.

He clamped and pulled, but the splinter head slipped right through his teeth. He moved the hand down where he could see it again. Derrick, who was humming louder now, and faster, whose head was still resting on Ben's shoulder, followed along with the light. Ben worked the flesh some more, got the thing to protrude just a little more, then brought the finger back up to his mouth and tried to make his mind a blank. But a blank mind was a luxury he doubted he'd ever attain again. Ruthie and Moon (whose given name was Mona; Moon was Ben's nickname for her) were always there, ready to replay their most scornful reactions to his endless failures.

He felt the thing yield, finally. He kept up the pressure, getting the splinter to where he could pull the rest out with his fingernails. Vince was holding still, barely breathing now. Afraid to breathe, most likely. Ben pulled slowly, carefully, making sure the splinter didn't break. "Holy shit," he said softly when it was out. "Holy shit." The thing had to have been a quarter of an inch long, maybe more. It looked like wood, though the taste in Ben's mouth had been slightly metallic—metal and dirt, and probably blood. He hocked up some phlegm to give weight to his saliva and spit as far as he could, his ball of sputum just clearing the edge of the ledge.

"Eww," Derrick said, a little boy stuck forever in an aging man's body.

Vince, who had withdrawn his hand, wiped the ooze from his finger on his baggy polyester shorts. Then he leaned in and looked at the splinter, still lying in the middle of Ben's palm, Derrick's light casting a nice yellow-white stage light over it. Vince said the same thing: "Holy shit." Then Derrick, who still had his head on Ben's shoulder, said it, which was funny because Derrick never cursed, even when Vince tried to bully him into it. The three of them had a laugh then—not a good one but a laugh nonetheless—and Ben thought that he and Vince were probably good again, and events from earlier in the day were already water under the bridge.

When Ben was half a block from the shelter, he put the carrier down under the shade of a coffee shop awning and put on his jacket and snapped it closed right up to his neck, leaving just a few snaps undone at his waistline. Then he took Siggy out of the carrier, and talking softly the whole time, explaining to Siggy what was about to happen, he stuffed him under his jacket on one side and then rolled the carrier up tight and stuffed it in on the other side. The jacket had a close-fitting ribbed bottom, but he would still need his arm to support Siggy's weight. Frank, the guy who manned the front desk, took his job seriously. Ben could only hope he wouldn't make anything of the fact that Ben was wearing a jacket in the middle of summer, a jacket bulging at the bottom. If he said something, Ben planned to say he was hauling a bunch of magazines that he wanted to look over now that he'd have access to artificial light, that it seemed easier to carry them in his jacket than keep the pile organized in his arms. In fact, he and his space mates did have a "library" out on the ledge, consisting of reading material they collected in their respective travels. Derrick didn't read but he liked pictures. Vince had four or five *National Geographics* that he read over and over again. And Ben had just recently scored a half-dozen outdated *New Yorkers* from the foot of a dumpster behind a suite of medical offices. If he had thought to bring along just one of them, he could have whipped it out of his jacket if Frank questioned him.

If he got caught trying to sneak a cat into the men's sleeping quarters, he'd lose his bed privilege; that was certain. Then he'd have to carry all his stuff, the sleeping bag and the trash bag and his backpack *and* the cat carrier, all the way back to the overpass, probably in the dark—which would be dangerous for a number of reasons, the rock squirrel holes the least among them—or try to find another place to spend the night, never a good idea, as you didn't want to unwittingly set down in someone else's territory. So when he came around the corner and saw that there was a crowd out in front of the shelter, that Frank was outside with everyone else huddled around two cars that looked to be totaled and staring in the direction of a third car, a police car down the road, he rather felt like he'd finally come up with a winning hand—an aberration in what had long been a losing streak.

He felt a tinge of guilt too, for feeling lucky at someone else's expense. But wasn't that the way it usually went? He glanced over at the accident scene as he passed behind it. The bigger car, a Taurus, had apparently gone through the stop sign and broadsided the smaller car, a late-model Prius the color of shiraz. He could tell who the victim was because the down-and-outers had mobilized around her, Angie and Jam glued to her sides like overly zealous Red Cross volunteers, their hands tight around her arms.

It was after five by then, so the men's dorm would be unlocked. All Ben had to do was get through the front door and he was home free. He could put Siggy back in the carrier and slide it between the wall and the cot. He'd stopped in the fields on the way over and walked Siggy on his leash until he'd done his business. Then he'd carried him in his arms for a while, so Siggy could look at him while he explained that he, Siggy, had to be extra quiet tonight. Now he was thinking that if no one else was around, he could leave Siggy inside for a minute or two and come back out and find out what was going on, what the police were doing at the other end of the street. There was something enticing about being a spectator at someone else's drama.

He pulled the door open and was just about to step in when the woman, the vic, twisted her head and looked right at him. He froze. He knew her, but from where? The way she squinted at him, the way she glared … Maybe, he thought, she was one of Ruthie's friends, or someone he'd met back before, someone who knew what he'd become. Or maybe she was just sizing him up because she sensed he was breaking the rules, dressed in the jacket in this heat. But why should she care? Luckily, just then he heard the ambulance approaching, and as if to further remind him that time was of the essence, Siggy, who had to be sweltering, slapped a paw on Ben's chest and spread his claws and left them that way. Ben moved forward and the door closed behind him.

3

LOLA

the puzzle

From her kitchen window Lola could see Janet across the street, locking the carved wooden gate set into the adobe wall that surrounded her house as far as the garage. That meant she was coming over. If she had been going somewhere in the car, she would be exiting *through* the garage, in her new hydro blue Wrangler Rubicon 392. Lola wasn't in the mood for her today, hadn't been since the accident.

The event the accident had triggered had actually made national news, but only for a short time. In the beginning it looked like Jamie Hernandez, who had been shot and killed by the police, would become the impetus for yet another uprising protesting police brutality against minorities. The narrative, initially, was that Hernandez had run along the side of a house to get away through its backyard, but when he saw there was a six-foot chain-link fence back there, he tried to get *inside* the house instead. The police were right behind him by then. They demanded he turn and put his hands in the air. He turned, but, according to the officer who shot him, instead of putting his hands up, he reached for something in the waistband of his pants.

The officer was wearing a body camera, but what happened next was obstructed by the hedges he was half hiding behind. Hernandez pulled out a knife, still in its leather sheath—not a gun. There was some controversy about the severity of the threat level of that the night the story broke. But the day after the woman who lived in the house told reporters and investigators she'd heard someone jiggling her side-door knob, and thinking it must be her neighbor, she'd opened the door a crack, and there was Hernandez, ready to push his way in, his knife—freed from its sheath by then—blazing in the late afternoon sun. She was horrified. If the officer hadn't shot just then, she insisted, Hernandez would have gotten in, and who knows what would have happened then. The story fizzled after that. "Fucker deserved it" continued to reflect the general consensus. That was basically Janet's take too.

Hernandez had done time some years back, for armed robbery, but if he'd really killed anyone to justify the teardrop tattoo near his eye, Lola had seen no mention of it in any of the news reports. She suspected he'd had the teardrop applied to make himself look meaner, as a way of protecting himself. Defense strategies were as crucial to survival in these times as they'd ever been, especially among those who felt most vulnerable. When an opossum felt threatened, it bared its teeth and foamed at the mouth and secreted a bad-smelling anal-gland fluid and became motionless, all to keep predators at bay. If Jamie Hernandez hadn't run down the street like someone with something to hide, people might be looking a little harder at the facts.

The whole thing troubled her. She couldn't help but feel that she was somehow responsible for the fact that Jamie Hernandez was dead. She wanted some quiet time to sort it out in her head. But she hadn't even been able to deal with the logistics that concerned *her* yet, the fact that she'd been in an accident, and until she reconciled with the insurance company—which couldn't seem to determine whether or not she had the right insurance to compensate for the fact that Hernandez's car had been uninsured—she didn't have a car to drive. But instead of peace and quiet, what she got was Janet. Janet daily, or nearly so. Janet seemed to like her best when she was at her worst.

Lola went into the living room and spoke to the dogs, who were at opposite ends of the sofa. "Janet is coming," she said firmly. "No barking." Blue, who was part husky, part lab—a gorgeous three-year-old with shortish cream-colored fur around his face (in the shape of a heart, no less) and lush tan everywhere else—jumped off the sofa at once and ran to the door barking madly. Well, Lola thought, at least he understood the part about someone coming.

"Quiet," Lola commanded. He glanced at her but continued to bark. In an effort to show him what was needed, Pete got down from the sofa and moved to the door and stood there, facing Lola, awaiting further instructions. "Good boy," Lola told him over Blue's yapping, and sure enough, Blue looked at Pete and quieted. Pete was a better trainer than she was, she concluded. In fact, Pete was nearly perfect. Lola had brought him in as a foster two years earlier, and within a week she knew she would never give him up. As for Blue, he had a couple of problems to overcome before she could start searching for a good home for him. One was the unnecessary barking. The other was chewing furniture legs when no one was around to deter him.

Lola took a deep breath and followed it with a forceful exhale. Then she threw the door open and Janet, who was just about to knock, marched in, wringing her hands and mumbling, "I've made a mistake. You're going to kill me." She went directly into the kitchen, where the two always sat when she visited. But the sight of the lime green hutch stopped her in her tracks. "Oh God!" Janet exclaimed. "What have you done to your beautiful hutch?"

Lola, who was forced to stop short behind her, made an effort to answer calmly. "Janet, you were here yesterday. You already told me what you think of it."

Janet turned to look at her, perplexed for a moment and then indignant. "What's your *point?* It's a disturbing color. I said so yesterday, and I'm saying it again today." She stepped to the round oak table in the middle of the room and plopped down in the same chair she always sat in, facing the refrigerator, the hutch to her right. "It's not personal. I can care about you and still hate your hutch." She straightened the edges of the placemat in front of her.

The *point* was that Janet had seen the hutch and commented on the color not only the day before but one other time that week. But this was probably not the time to try to talk to her about what Lola believed could be a memory loss issue.

Mostly Janet's memory lapses seemed to be in regard to particular items, unimportant things. Like umbrellas. She'd called one day when it was supposed to rain to ask Lola if she could borrow her umbrella. Lola asked what happened to *her* umbrella, the mauve-colored one she kept in the big basket by her front door with her yoga mats. It wasn't a big deal, but then two days later Janet called with the same question—and got the same answer. Another time it was about Lola's porcelain tea kettle. It caught Janet's eye as soon as she walked into the kitchen that day, and she went right over to it and picked it up and marveled over how pretty it was, the artwork, the tree and the little robins flying in circles around it. "When did you get this?" Janet had cried, and Lola had to remind her that she'd had it for years, that it was always right there on the counter, a showpiece she never used.

Lola had suggested once before that Janet might want to consider seeing someone, in case her memory lapses indicated a more serious condition that could be nipped in the bud. But Janet insisted she would be the one to know if there was a real problem; they were her wheels after all, and she could feel them turning as fast as ever. She was simply experiencing occasional bouts of amnesia—transient global amnesia, to be precise. She'd researched it on the internet. It was actually fairly common and would likely go away by itself. Lola agreed that her analysis was probably correct, but all the more reason to see someone for confirmation. But if some so-called medical professional got it wrong and misdiagnosed her, Janet had argued, she could potentially fall under the spell of their inaccurate conclusion, which could result in a call for an incorrect medication, which in turn could bring about the worsening of her condition, not to mention the possibility of a multitude of side effects. All she needed was a rebalancing of her diet and some lifestyle tweaks. Less wine and pot, more yoga. Maybe some green tea supplements. Or apple cider vinegar. She'd figure it out. She didn't want to hear Lola's or anyone else's opinion about it.

But not all Janet's lapses were about umbrellas and tea kettles and repainted furniture. Janet was loaded; when she was very young she'd married her boss, an art dealer in New York who also played the stock market. Among other intuitive purchases, he'd bought quite a lot of Apple back in 1980 when it was $22 a share. When they divorced, he kept their loft apartment in Manhattan and Janet got almost all the stocks.

Janet didn't have kids of her own, but as each of her sister Francine's children went off to college, Janet gave them a sum of money. But when the youngest, Liz, got accepted into a college and called Janet to collect, Janet insisted she had never promised any money to her. She called Liz a liar and a scam artist and hung up on her. Francine called back, screaming that Liz had run out of the house crying and had taken off in the family car. If anything happened to her, it would be Janet's fault. Finally, Bart, Francine and Janet's older brother, had to get involved, and somehow the problem got resolved.

Lola, who knew everyone in Janet's family, learned about this whole ugly incident not from Janet but from Francine. Francine had called after the dust settled, wanting to know if Lola had noticed anything weird going on with her sister. This was before the umbrella and the tea kettle and now the hutch, so Lola said no. Now she didn't know what to do. It was one more thing to think about—if she ever found the space.

Lola sighed and went to the stove to heat up coffee for the two of them. When it was ready, she sat down across from her friend, sighed again, and said, "So, tell me about the mistake you made, the one I'm going to kill you for." She forced a smile.

Lola and Janet had lived across the street from each other as kids back in Hudson, Ohio. They had walked to school together, all through grammar school and junior high. They'd hung out with the same group of friends all those years too, namely other kids from their neighborhood. But once they got into high school, they made new friends and weren't together so much anymore. They stayed in touch over the years, though—through college, through four marriages (three of them Janet's), through the birth of one kid (Lola's), and the loss of that same kid as well as the loss of all four of their parents—with letters and emails and by phone, and, regarding the weddings and funerals, visits. What they shared, mainly, was a long history, and what they focused on when they wrote to each other were the inflection points in their lives that would be added to it. But then nine years ago, when Lola turned forty-eight and George, her then husband, left, Janet, who was recently divorced herself, came out to New Mexico to help Lola get back on her feet—though Lola had never asked for any help. And Janet never left! She lived in an apartment in Santa Fe for the first year or so, and when the house across the street from Lola went on the market, Janet bought it—and quickly brought it up to her standards with room extensions and enlarged windows and kiva fireplaces and vigas and latillas and lots of stone work and the six-foot high adobe wall to hold it all together. So here they were, living the same distance from each other as they had when they were kids.

Janet straightened and spit it out. "I mentioned your ordeal on Facebook."

"What do you mean?"

She put her cup down and shook her head side to side. "This whole thing. The guy who broadsided you, what happened to him, the toll it's taken on you ..."

Lola used Facebook for her dog training and grooming business, but she didn't have a personal account. She didn't understand the ramifications of what Janet was saying to her. "Okay," she began slowly. "Well, I guess I'm not going to kill you, Janet. Maim you maybe." She laughed, but Janet only stared back at her. "I mean, it was in all the papers anyway. It's not like you divulged a secret." She picked up her cup and took a sip. "Of course I would prefer you didn't talk about my personal response. Though I don't see why anyone would even be interested."

"Lolo, you don't understand how Facebook works. Half my friends are people you know, from when we were kids. Now they're all contacting me to ask for your phone number or email so they can—"

"You didn't give it to anyone, did you?" Lola interrupted. She hated when Janet called her Lolo.

"'Course not," Janet mumbled, but then she looked aside, her gaze sweeping over a section of the tiled floor. It was exactly what the dogs did when Lola reprimanded them for something.

"Please don't give my number or email out to anyone. I don't care who it is. I don't want to talk to anyone from our school days right now. Or probably ever. Do you understand? And please don't mention me anymore on Facebook."

Minutes passed, the two women alternating between sipping their coffees and staring into their cups. Finally Lola glanced at the clock and mumbled, "I have a Shepherd coming in a few minutes, for grooming."

"I really don't want to leave like this, with you mad at me."

"I'm not mad at you, Janet. You told me what you did. I asked you not to do it again. It's over. We don't have a problem. And you have to leave, whether you want to or not. I've got work."

Janet got up and put her empty cup in the sink. But instead of leaving, she mulled around, stopping to look at pictures Lola had stuck on her refrigerator door with magnets over the years, most yellowed with age and curling at the unsecured corners. As if she were seeing them for the first time, she made comments: *Val looks so pretty here.* Valerie had been Lola's daughter. *That was when she first started the diet*, Lola mumbled. *Oh, and look at George. So handsome.* Lola nodded. Their exchange went on for another moment or two, lifeless.

In the other room, Blue heard the car turn into the driveway and jumped from the sofa and ran to the door, barking again. Pete got up as well and watched for Lola to come through the archway from the kitchen. When she did, she nodded at him and then jutted her chin toward the door, and knowing exactly what she wanted, he added his own deep bark to Blue's yappy one. Janet, just emerging from the kitchen herself, put her hands over her ears. Her mouth was open and moving, but Lola couldn't hear her over the dogs. She turned her palms up, confirming helplessness. Lola opened the door, and Janet, who was shaking her head in frustration, quickly exited. Lola closed the door behind her and said "stop," and both dogs did. "Good boys," she said, looking at Blue. He was getting it, finally. She dug some treats out of her pocket. "Sit," she said. They both sat and Lola gave them a few more. Then she went into the dining room and exited through the door there and went to meet her client, Dolores, and Rex, her dog, outside by the shop.

Dolores opted not to hang around and wait for Rex; she had grocery shopping to do, she said. Surely she had heard about the accident, but she didn't mention it. Lola appreciated that. "Come on, Rex," she said, and she walked him toward the larger of her two stainless steel bathing tubs. Three hours later, he had had a bath, blow dry, brushing, rear-end trim and anal gland expression, nail trim, and ear and teeth cleaning. Lola left him in the shop (he was aggressive with other dogs) and went into the house to find her cell phone so she could call Dolores to come and get him. After they disconnected, she listened to the voicemail Janet had left: *There's more. I tried to tell you before but the conversation didn't go right. Call me when your client leaves. I need to tell you before it's too late.*

Lola shook her head. There was always *more* with Janet. Situations developed and never ended. She glanced out her kitchen window, at the pet cemetery at the back of her property. Over the years she had buried six dogs and two cats in an area off to the side of the shed at the very back of her property. Both cats and three of the dogs had lived their lives with Lola and George. The fourth dog Lola had adopted after George left, and she had died only the previous year. The other two dogs had belonged to clients, both people who lived in apartments and who had asked Lola to let them bury their beloved pups on her property so that they could visit them occasionally. Eventually Lola put up a white picket fence to mark the area and a small wooden sign that said *Pet Cemetery.* She had painted it herself. She also had workers come by and remove the old shed and replace it with a new one. She painted it white to match the fence.

Lola hit a few icons on her phone, one of them *speaker*, and held it up and let the message play through once more, this time for Blue and Pete. They cocked their heads at the sound of Janet's familiar whining. "What are we going to do with her?" Lola asked them.

Lola rolled her eyes to the ceiling. Janet was such a drama queen; she always had been, since they were little girls. She went out to the shop to wait with Rex for Dolores, and once they were gone she returned to the house and called Janet, and as Janet didn't answer, she left her a message: *My client's gone. You can come back if you want. I'll put some fresh coffee on.* She followed her declaration with a loud sigh. She couldn't help herself. She found herself sighing all the time when Janet was around. She opened the front door, so that Blue would see Janet coming through the screen door and refrain from barking. Then she went into the kitchen to put the coffee on. In no time Janet, who let herself in, was there, peeking around the archway, a smile on her pink face, a twinkle in her eye. "Does this mean you're not mad anymore?" she asked, childlike.

"It means I'm well mannered. You wanted to say more, and I'm prepared to hear you out. You have the floor." Her words were meant to be lighthearted. Her mood had picked up some. Rex was a good boy, calm and thoughtful. She'd pretty much told him everything that was going on in her life while she worked on him. Dogs were less nervous during the grooming process when the groomer spoke to them continuously, in a soft monotone, which is how she spoke anyway. And it was good for her. Self-talk helped her to work through problems and make decisions and get things done that she might otherwise put off. And maybe Rex and the other pups she worked with understood some of what she said. Dogs understood a lot more than people gave them credit for, in her opinion.

Janet brushed the lime green hutch with her hand as she was going for her chair. She withdrew it quickly.

"Stop that," Lola snapped. But then she chuckled. Janet was so predictable.

Janet sat. She waited a beat and then asked, cheerfully, "Does Pete have a gun?"

Lola looked back from the counter. She shook her head. She could only imagine where this was going.

Janet shot a look at Pete, out on the sofa in the other room. The big brown bullmastiff mix anticipated Lola's every move. Janet often joked that she wished she could find a man like him. "While I was waiting for you to call back I read that a dog in Arizona shot his master with a rifle."

"Oh, Janet," Lola said, but she felt the giddiness rising.

"I swear. The rifle was in the bed of his truck and the dog hopped up and stepped on it and set it off somehow and the bullet hit the guy. The guy didn't have the safety on. The bullet went into his arm, in one side and out the other. The sheriff said that he'd been in law enforcement for more than forty years and this was the first case he'd ever had where a dog shot his owner."

Lola put the cups on the table. "This was in the news?"

Janet threw her palms out. "On Facebook. I thought you'd like it since you love dogs and hate men. You don't know what you're missing, Lolo. You know, there are even dating sites on Facebook."

Lola tossed her head back. "I don't hate men, Janet. And if you really believed I did, why would you think I'd want to look at a dating site? Do you see the contradiction there?"

"I'm trying to warm you up," Janet admitted.

"Because this additional thing you're going to tell me will be that bad?"

"Well, not as bad as having your own dog shoot you." She looked again at Pete, and as if he were psychic, he lifted his head and stared back at her, alert.

Lola sat down and observed her friend evenly over her cup. When she was mad at Janet, which was much of time, she dwelled on the fact that they had so little in common.

Lola had a small footprint. She tried not to buy anything she didn't really need. Janet was always buying new clothes, new jewelry, new furniture. She was also basically apolitical. She didn't seem to care that they were living through the beginning of the end of democracy, or worse, the end of times. To be apolitical in such times, in Lola's mind, was to be complicit in all the evil going on in the world. It was worse than being apolitical in Hitler's Germany because on top of all the evil actors, all the truth deniers, now there was climate crisis too, and the ongoing viral outbreaks, and dictatorships popping up all over the place. And now it even looked like there was the potential for a third world war, *now*, when there were so many nuclear weapons out there. How could anyone be apolitical?

When Lola talked about politics, Janet complained that she was exhausting. Once Lola had replied that it couldn't be more exhausting than listening to Janet talk about clothes. They hadn't spoken for a few days after that. When she first came to New Mexico, Janet said she hated the desert. She complained that everything was dusty and beige-colored. But then she'd changed her tune. Why? Not because she had come to cherish the rich beauty of the desert, the way the morning sunlight turned plants and trees to gold, the frenzied colors that waltzed through the evening sky, but because she liked the architecture and décor she'd discovered living among the affluent in Santa Fe. *Don't judge*, Lola said to herself. *Just don't judge.*

"You hear about Kim Kardashian?" Janet went on, deadpan.

Lola began to laugh. She couldn't help herself. But she didn't want to hear about Kim Kardashian right now. She remembered she had cupcakes, and she got up and went to the hutch and retrieved a plastic dinner plate covered with aluminum foil. Janet watched her with her eyes shielded, as if from the sight of the hutch itself. "I still can't believe you did that," Janet mumbled. "Makes me sick."

Lola placed the plate on the table. "Try one. Mrs. Quick made them, to cheer me up after ..."

"The neighbor to the south, the old lady with all the property and nice trees?"

"The very same. She's very sweet and very lonely." Lola sighed.

"Who isn't?" Janet quipped.

"She's having her property subdivided, you know."

"There goes the neighborhood."

"It won't be so bad. The part she's subdividing is way off the road. I guess she wants to build another house back there. She'll have to have a road put in for anyone to reach it. She talks so fast, and she runs from one subject to another and doesn't give you a minute to ask a question." Lola removed the tin foil. On the plate were four vanilla cupcakes with turquoise-colored frosting and some kind of blackish-green gummy-looking candy on top. Lola, who hadn't had one yet, who was seeing them for the first time herself, was astonished. It was unfathomable how unappetizing they looked.

For a moment both women were speechless. Then Janet whispered, "Oh. My. God. That's bird shit on top." She glanced at the hutch, as if making a comparison in her mind. Then she got up so suddenly that at first Lola thought she was going to be sick. But she only dashed the two or three steps to the refrigerator and threw the door open. And there she stood, staring for a while before she retrieved a jar of assorted olives and brought it back to the table. She removed the lid and stuck her fingers in and popped the olive she'd seized into her mouth.

George used to say that Janet had a problem recognizing boundaries. That was certainly true. Lola had been an only child, an only child living with a divorced mom whose mission in life was to teach Lola perfect manners. George had been an only child too. Janet had four siblings, two of them boys. Boundaries went out the window when you grew up in a big household like that.

But the truth was, Lola admired Janet immeasurably for being able to open her refrigerator like that and take what she wanted, without asking, without giving it a second thought.

These days Lola was working on pushing through her own boundaries. That's why she'd painted the hutch such a bright color. She'd read somewhere about a fairy tale describing a farming village experiencing severe drought. With their crops all but dead, the village elders sent one of their members on a long journey to meet with a shaman to ask him what to do, and the shaman said they should paint, paint their houses, inside and out, paint everything beautiful bright colors. The villagers did so, and thereafter it began to rain, and the crops began to grow again.

After George left, which was shortly after Valerie died, Lola had unplugged from everything but work and, of course—necessarily since she'd imposed herself in Lola's small world—Janet. But recently Lola had come to feel enough was enough; it was time to embark on a new path for whatever time she had left on the planet. Painting the hutch was her way of telling the universe to feel free to pitch in, do its share of the work, illuminate this new path if it was so inclined, so that maybe Lola could find the damn thing.

All at once Lola was filled with love for the chubby pink bunny of a woman sitting across from her, eating all her olives straight from the jar with her fingers. She reached across the table. She wanted to take Janet's free hand, squeeze it before the feeling fled and she found herself wishing Janet a good life in a nice house a thousand miles away again. But Janet misunderstood and slid the jar toward her groping fingers. "All right, I'm just going to come right out and say this and get it over with," she said. She leaned toward the kitchen cabinets and stretched out her arm and wiped the fingertips of her right hand—the ones that had been in the olive jar—on the tea towel that was hanging from one of the upper draw pulls. "I told you I mentioned it, your ordeal, on Facebook."

"Un huh," Lola said, withdrawing her hand and marveling that Janet managed to discuss the accident without ever actually saying the word.

"Well, George was one of the people who saw what I posted." She took a breath. Then she took a sip from her coffee cup. "This is cold," she said to no one as she pushed the cup aside.

Lola wondered what George was doing on Janet's Facebook. Though she was not about to ask, she had to know *now*, immediately, what it was that Janet was going to confess regarding George, and until she knew she would remain just as she was, suspended in dread, a helpless pupa dangling from a tree twig.

"I hope you're not upset he's on my Facebook. I can see by your face, which kind of looks like granite right now ..."

Lola tried to shake her head to the contrary, but she didn't have the mobility to manage it.

"Lolo, I have over five hundred friends. It's not like we discuss you. I *like* his photographs of palm trees on the beach and he *likes* my *American's Got Talent* videos. That constitutes friendship in these times, though you wouldn't know that since you're above it all. Anyway, George saw, from my post, that you were having a hard time and he called me—I didn't even realize my number was listed, but he found it somewhere—and … Well, I never talked to him. I didn't recognize *his* number so of course I didn't answer the phone. I swear I get fifty spam calls a day. But he left a message. He said he was worried about you, that he'd been thinking a lot about you lately, just having a bad feeling that you were in trouble."

Janet slapped both her chubby little hands down on the table and looked at them for a beat or two. "Bottom line, he's coming out here. He said not to tell you. He wants to surprise you. But I figured you'd never speak to me again if I didn't give you some warning. He asked if I could put him up for a few days. I guess he doesn't know I live right across the street." She chuckled. "I texted back that he could stay with me if he wants. What else was I going to do? You would have done the same had it been any of mine. Then I thought better of it. You're not me. You're not so open like that. But by then it was too late. I'd already clicked *send*. You know how that goes." She shrugged. "Maybe you don't. Anyway, so, I guess we'll have George to kick around in good time." She smiled, but Lola didn't smile back.

"Call him," Lola said evenly. "Tell him not to come."

She left Janet in the kitchen and walked stiffly through the living room and into her bedroom and sat on the edge of her bed, facing her chest of drawers. On top of the chest—splayed open, its gold cover with its wreath of tiny pink and blue flowers—was her memory book, where she had been recording everything she could remember about her daughter for the last ten years. How pitiful it was that there was only one volume, and still plenty of blank pages at the back. Yes, it was a thick book, and Lola's writing was tiny, but it still pained her to acknowledge that whole days of her time with Valerie were lost forever.

When she couldn't think of something new to add to the book, she read entries she'd written previously. Just that morning, she'd reread the entry she'd entitled *Hawk*. When Valerie was thirteen, she'd walked to the local park to meet up with some girls from the neighborhood. After a few hours, everyone dispersed in a different direction, heading to their respective homes for dinner. Valerie was just making her way between two tall ponderosa pines when a hawk, screeching ferociously, swooped down out of nowhere and came within inches of attacking her before it swooped away again.

She burst into the house crying, her hand over her mouth, her eyes wide with terror. George had been filling the dogs' food bowls, and I was just setting the table. We dropped what we were doing and ran to her. Her pain, her terror, it was awful. I thought the worst. I thought she'd been attacked, by a man. I was looking at her clothes, for signs. I was breathing hard, blood pumping through my body. I was ready to run out and kill whoever it was, if I could only find him. Finally she calmed enough to speak. A hawk. We looked at each other over her head. Only a hawk, thank God. But still. George said it had to have had babies nearby, otherwise … but Val said no, it was her, the hawk had singled her out because she was fat and stupid and no one liked her. Why else would a hawk attack a girl walking home for dinner? That night, after we were sure she was asleep, we talked about it, how to get her to love herself.

We let her stay home from school the next day, and we both canceled whatever we had to. George found two umbrellas in the back of the closet, and the three of us walked to the park with her between us, the umbrellas overlapping over her head. We stood between the two trees, where she was the day before, George looking through his binoculars for the nest while Val clutched my arm, and turned her head from side to side, as if anticipating another attack. Finally George spotted the nest.

He gave me the binoculars and showed me where to look. It was almost impossible to see anything at first. The nest was really high up, huge, a blast of twigs of all sizes. Inside it was one full-size hawk—the mother, the hen, it must have been, and two small hawks, eyas. You could barely see their heads above that wild splay of twigs. Maybe there were more than two, but two was all we could see from below.

We had to promise to be on the lookout for the father hawk to get Val to look through the binoculars herself. But once she did, she watched for a long time, in utter silence, right until someone on the street behind us started a motorcycle and startled her. Then she was done. She pushed the binoculars back at her father. She wanted to go home, right then, before the tiercel, who was probably out hunting, returned. Babies, *George said on the way back, his arm slung around her shoulders.* We all do what we think is necessary to protect our babies. *She rolled her eyes at him.*

She was quiet the rest of the day, pensive. I could tell by the set of her mouth that she was still upset. But she didn't say anything more about the incident and George and I didn't either. Then the next day, she came home from school happy again, or as happy as she ever got in those last years. Mrs. S, her favorite teacher, a Native woman who taught language arts, told her seeing a hawk was a good thing, though she conceded that no one wanted to see one that close or that suddenly. Hawks represented strength and courage and honesty and clear vision. Mrs. S said her ancestors believed they were messengers. She gave Val the choice of doing whatever homework assignment the rest of the class would be doing that night or finding a poem about hawks and reading it for the class the next day.

The three of us spent the evening combing through the poetry books we had right there on our own shelves. Many of the hawk poems we found were about death, hawks as skilled killers. George and I didn't even call her attention to those. But then she found one herself, by Henry David Thoreau. It was very short, which was perfect, because Valerie had never liked to be center stage. The three of us interpreted it together. It seemed to say that if you stayed engaged with life, the way hawks did, you could waive pain—waive, Thoreau's word.

4

BEN

rota fortunae

Ben had planned to sit there on his cot until the room filled, because it was less likely that anyone would bother to rustle through his things in a full room. But he was still the only one there. He could see from the window across from him that the accident that had allowed him to slip inside unseen—if you didn't count the vic, who had looked right at him—was still holding everyone's attention. The vic was gone now—an ambulance had taken her away—but the down-and-outers who'd witnessed the event seemed to be doing a meet and greet with the new arrivals, each relaying his or her version of the story. When you were a down-and-outer you could go days with nothing new to talk about. Maybe, he began to think, *this* was the time to make his move. Quickly, he dug clean clothes out of his trash bag (he'd done his wash at the Laundromat the week before) and hurried down the stairs into the basement to the men's shower room, which he'd used only a few times previously, because if you weren't staying for the night, you could only sign up for a shower once every two weeks.

There were five shower heads along one wall, each about three feet apart. He picked the one in the middle and ran the water while he stripped. He noticed he was losing weight, but he wasn't going to ponder the ramifications of that just now. He was still feeling lucky; he'd rolled a seven; he wasn't about to let anything convince him otherwise.

It was dangerous to think in terms of luck; he knew that better than anyone. He'd thought himself lucky the night he'd gone into Gino's—because Ruthie was in one of her moods and wouldn't stop nagging and at least he had a place to go, close enough that he could walk there—and look how that turned out; it was the worst night of his life. But stepping into the steaming shower, he couldn't help but think his hunch about this moment was genuine. He was in the shelter; he'd *got* in without anyone seeing Sig; and now he had a hot shower all to himself—in a shower room that had been packed full the other times he'd been there—without having to worry about anyone touching his stuff, all because of someone else's misfortune, the woman who'd been t-boned. That was how the wheel of fortune worked; Fortuna's spin landed one person up at the top of the wheel while another got pushed below. He washed his hair quickly but thoroughly—with his own shampoo, one of those mini plastic bottles that Ruthie had saved from some hotel they'd stayed at years back, when they'd had the money to travel occasionally—and soaped up with a partially used bar from the aluminum basket on the wall. He dried off and dressed and hurried back to his cot.

Luck remained at his side. He was still the only one there. He flung himself down on the cot the way a child might. Then he rolled over and dipped his head to check on Siggy. Siggy opened his mouth in a silent meow, and Ben silent-meowed back at him. Then he dug his smart phone and charger out of his backpack and plugged them into the outlet on the wall. It had been a while since he'd had a charged phone. He'd tried to charge it in the Laundromat while he was waiting for his clothes to spin dry, but the attendant, a girl about seventeen, explained that phone charging wasn't allowed, and he could see in her eyes that she was terrified he might argue with her, so he pulled the charger out of the wall.

His phone was a freebee on Ruthie's plan. Since it didn't cost her any extra, she hadn't taken him off yet. But one of these days she would, either because her anger remained unmanageable or because it was no longer free. He figured it would hold a charge for at least two days. And he'd be clean that long too. Tomorrow morning he'd go online first thing and look for a job, before Fortuna got anywhere near her wheel. And he'd find one, because he had to.

A true streak of good luck needed a name, he decided: *Shiraz,* the color of the car the perp had totaled. It had a magical sound to it. He waved his hand in the air as if it were a wand. "Shiraz," he said in his best wizard voice. And just then the door opened, and Dolly stuck her head in and said, "Dinner's going to be late, because of the scene out there. You want I should fix you a snack to tide you over?"

Ben could have cried, he was so happy in that moment. He was starving. "Thank you, Dolly. You are a wonderful young woman."

Dolly smiled and retreated.

Ben had just finished the ham sandwich Dolly brought him when the men began drifting in. Following a few brief exchanges with the ones who took the cots nearest to him, he rolled toward the wall and pretended to be falling asleep. The men whose numbers Dolly had called that morning, and again at lunch time, had until 8:00 P.M. to show up and claim their prize. After that securing one of the remaining cots depended on where you were on the line that formed outside the building. There were women on the line too, waiting for a shot at one of the beds in the women's section. This particular shelter didn't allow kids.

Sometimes fights broke out on the line. Last week, Ben had heard, someone had gotten as far as the door when Frank came out and said they were all full. The man next on line, an older guy who was somewhat hunched, straightened enough to punch old Frank in the face and make his nose bleed. The guy had been participating in the drawings for months and had never once had his number called; nor had he ever been able to get to the front of the line in time to get one of the remaining beds. Now he was prohibited from ever showing himself at the shelter again. That meant he was going to have to resettle near one of the other shelters, all miles apart in different directions. It meant starting all over with figuring out a system—where to get food, where to relieve himself, and so on. It would be a challenge for a guy like him, an older fellow who didn't move very fast. It could easily be the beginning of the end.

By 9:00 P.M. the room was full and everyone was settling in. There was a nightlight on near the door, but the overhead had been turned off. There was still some chat going on, but not too much. All the men had brought their odors in with them, and Ben, who didn't smoke, could smell cigarettes— and booze and of course body odor. The noise level actually increased over the next hour, because as the men fell off to sleep they began snoring or groaning or farting, or executing combinations thereof.

Ben awoke in the middle of the night and saw that the moon outside the nearby window was waning gibbous. It had been years since he'd paid any attention to the phases of the moon, but now, since he'd become a down-and-outer, he was always aware of them. He was aware from a practical sense—a fuller moon meant more people mulling around in the dark when he was out in the field near the ledge, often louder, more agitated, more aggressive, more chance of being bit by a rat or a stray dog—as well as aesthetically; the light of the full moon, he'd (re)discovered, was purely awesome. The sight of the full moon, or any moon really, up in the night sky, made him think in phrases these days, fragments of poems he'd read long ago, or phrases that simply came into his head out of nowhere, as if *he* were a poet, or a song-writer unconsciously sifting through all the words in the world to find the ones that would best unearth his own deepest thoughts and emotions. He only wished he'd paid attention to the moon before now, that he'd shared his moon-inspired thoughts with Ruthie, that he'd taken the time to write her poems, even if they weren't very good. Maybe she would have loved him better. Maybe she would have loved him just enough to forgive him.

He was always aware of the weather now too, the slight fluctuations in temperature, the shifts in the direction of the wind. He'd become addicted to the sky, which was a deep mesmerizing blue most days but turned a fiery red or orange at dusk and dawn. He watched the cloud formations, the way the clouds crawled over the peaks of mountains off to the east—or sometimes consumed them, wiping them clear off the canvas for a time. He made a study of the three volcanoes, "the three sisters," off to the west, of how following the smooth line from one to another calmed him when he was agitated. When he walked, he noticed the smallest things, the paint peeling into a soft curl at the edge of a shop door, the loose sole on the shoe of the man walking in front of him … He had lost so much in such a short time, and his losses were a hole in his heart, a crater in his soul. But there were times, like now, when he experienced immense gratitude for what remained, the moment he found himself in—the moonlight, the cot, the pillow, a showered body, the breakfast he would have in the morning, the door on the toilet stall where he would sit and have himself a proper shite, the phone that would be fully charged and holding the information he needed to regain his footing.

He stretched his arm between his cot and the wall and poked the mesh screen at the front of Siggy's carrier until he found a body part, a paw tip, which Siggy quickly withdrew. *Shiraz*, he whispered, an exhale that no one could have heard. *Shiraz*, because Siggy was alive and so was he, and the moonlight had turned all the down-and-outers in the room—himself included—into silver angels with untroubled hearts, grateful for this shared respite from whatever they'd suffered during this day and were likely to suffer tomorrow. His eyelids fluttered. *Shiraz*, he whispered once more, and all at once he remembered where he'd met her, the woman from the accident.

Jim Hanson's son Brian had gotten his degree in veterinary medicine. The party was for him. The woman—he couldn't remember her name; probably he hadn't bothered to ask—was there because of something to do with animals.

He'd gone to the bar Jim had set up in the dining room to get more wine for Ruthie and himself, and he'd noticed her standing there, alone, looking uncomfortable. She was tall and lanky—like Olive Oyl, he'd thought at the time—with pin-straight medium blond hair cut to chin length and pushed behind her ears. Oversized glasses, with light blue plastic frames, he remembered, pretty much the same shade as her eyes. Unlike most of the other female partygoers, who'd dressed up some for the occasion, she was wearing jeans, with a white cotton button-down shirt and tiny dangling turquoise earrings. He smiled at her, and she smiled back, but then she tucked her head and looked aside. He poured the wine into the two glasses he'd carried in from the other room, and as he was passing her, he stopped to ask if she was a friend of Nadine, Jim's ex-wife. Nadine had brought along a posse of friends to help her deal with the fact that she had to be in the same house as Jim for the sake of their son. But the woman said no, she didn't know Nadine. Her connection was to Brian, something about a dog advocacy organization, he remembered now.

She was odd, he thought at the time. Early fifties, he surmised, but she could have been a schoolgirl the way her eyes darted away from his after every landing, the way her hand jerked when she reached to push back a loose strand of hair. He turned his head to look over his shoulder, into the living room. Ruthie was holding forth in there at the center of a circle that included Jim and Beth, Jim's new, much younger wife, and a few others. She was talking about the heat in the salsa they'd had at Papa Felipe's, a restaurant they'd gone to recently. She had an appetizer of some sort balanced on a cocktail napkin on her palm, which she held out flat, like a waitress carrying someone's miniature tray. She was wearing a plain blue dress she'd worn many times before but somehow she looked overdressed in it now that she dyed her hair a ginger color, to hide the gray that was starting to come in.

He turned back to the stranger. "You want to come and join us?" He tilted his head toward his wife and the others.

"Thank you," she said. "I will. I'll come by in just a minute."

He nodded, smiled once more, and returned to Ruthie's side and handed her her wine. When he thought to look back a few moments later, the woman was gone.

Ben hated to go back to the ledge in the morning, but once he'd eaten and used the bathroom, there was no place else to go; the shelter didn't allow people to hang out between meals. He left when everyone else did, and because everyone was carrying something, no one noticed that his sleeping bag was folded over a cat carrier.

Getting through town and across the rock squirrel fields with all his possessions and Siggy in his carrier was a challenge, but he refused to focus on it. He planned to get right down to it—to find a job, any job, right away. The last time he'd been clean and had a charged phone, he hadn't even gotten an interview, because he'd been looking for a real job, something that would pay fairly well, be halfway interesting, and get him back on the path to the lifestyle he'd enjoyed previously. He hadn't planned to tell the people he talked to that he was homeless, but they got suspicious when he couldn't explain why he'd left his previous job, couldn't give them an address or guarantee they would reach him if they tried to call him back in a day or two, couldn't promise he would be clean enough to come in for an interview if they couldn't see him right away. Keeping yourself presentable day after day was impossible when you were homeless.

Now he knew better. Once you were homeless, you had to crawl your way back to your vision of a real life in increments. The only requirements he had now were that his job be near a bus route and that it pay enough that he could get a room somewhere. The size of a closet would work out just fine. All he needed was a place where he and Siggy could get a good night's sleep, use a bathroom—a share would work—store his things, and leave for work with a clean shirt on his back and enough change in his pocket for a sandwich at some point during the day. He had to find something. Summer would be over soon, and he was not going to be homeless through the winter. Siggy would never survive it.

In his previous life Ben had been an architect, working as part of a team to generate designs for local health care and social service clinics. After some thirty-plus years in Albuquerque, he'd built a reputation within the health and well-being community. He'd worked for a company called Telini Industries, but it was his name, Ben Frey, that came up when plans were being made to build new facilities or add wings to existing ones. In fact, he'd even designed one of the city's homeless shelters some years ago, never thinking he would become a frequent visitor to another of them.

His stint in jail lasted three days. When the police stormed Gino's, there were only three people there: the bartender/owner, who was losing his mind because of all the broken chairs and glass and blood all over the place; the guy bleeding out on the floor; and Ben, confused as hell and bleeding himself, wearing his shirt tied around his head. The ambulance was on its way by then, but two of the cops yelled for towels and went to work trying to stop the dying guy's blood flow. The other two cops questioned the bartender, asking *if this guy here*, meaning Ben, was the one who'd beaten the dying guy to pulp, and the bartender said yes! Later he would come to his senses and explain that yes, Ben was one of the people who'd been in the brawl that resulted in one guy dead (he died on his way to the hospital in the ambulance) and the near-destruction of his bar, but he couldn't say for certain that Ben was *the* one who started everything, let alone that he was the one who'd clobbered the dead guy. Really, it could have been anyone.

But the ball was in motion by then. Thanks to a couple of earnest reporters who made it to Gino's nearly as quickly as the police, everyone in Albuquerque had already seen the footage of two cops dragging a highly resistive, cussing (frankly, he was still drunk), handcuffed, bare-chested man out of the bar and pushing him into the squad car. He was still wearing his shirt on his head. Though his head wound turned out to be fairly superficial, the shirt was full of blood, and blood had run down his face and back and chest. One news anchor quipped that the last time she'd seen anything *that* scary-looking, she'd been in a movie theater watching *Spree*, and her co-anchor—who was happy to identify Ben and say where he worked and mention the names of his wife and daughter—laughed outright.

When he showed up at work the next week, Buster Telini told him to take some time off, and when he called around to some of the people he knew in the business, to see if they might have some odd jobs for him in the meantime, they said virtually the same thing. Okay, he thought, it was still all manageable. He would have his day in court and be proven innocent, and the image that had been stamped in the heads of all the people who had caught his TV debut would eventually fade. He'd been an optimist back then. And he'd been wrong.

5

LOLA

the gambit

The house was a small adobe-style cottage separated from its neighbors on both sides by a chain-link fence. While there was no landscaping to speak of—nothing but a few anemic-looking shrubs and some rocks left from what had likely been an effort at xeriscaping years earlier—the place looked tidy enough, especially considering the state of some of the houses surrounding it. The one on the left had an old mattress leaning up against it and two beat-up-looking cars up on blocks in the front yard. The one on the right had badly peeling paint and cardboard taped over the single-pane windows, one piece of which featured a hand-drawn message about the availability of Mary Kay products.

Lola turned off the ignition and took a deep breath. The vehicle she was driving, a white 2006 Chevrolet van, felt like a tank after her Prius. As it had only front and back windows, she'd turned down Janet's invitation to meet for lunch downtown afterwards, because the parking lots there were always full and she wasn't ready to try to parallel park the thing out on the street. It looked like a Roto Rooter van to her; she hated it. But it had belonged to someone she knew, a single owner who had retired from his construction job, and it was clean and the mileage was low and the price was right. And, most importantly, it would work much better for transporting dogs than the Prius ever had. It only had seats in the front, so Lola could even fill it up with crates if she needed to. But she was already wondering how expensive it would be to turn the back into a mini grooming salon, so that she could make house calls.

Lola was used to going into the homes of strangers, but this time, the stranger whose door she was about to knock on wasn't expecting her, and she was a jangle of nerves. She knocked lightly at first, thinking that it wasn't too late to turn and flee. But then she made herself knock again, harder, because if she didn't do this now, it would only be even more difficult the next time she tried.

Lola heard footsteps and straightened. The door opened a couple of inches. A chain kept it from opening farther. An older Latino woman, perhaps in her early eighties, leaned over her walker. "Mrs. Hernandez?" Lola asked.

The woman only stared back at her.

"I'm sorry to bother you. I was there, at the accident."

Still the woman said nothing. Her eyes, Lola thought, could have been pistol barrels.

"I know you lost your son." She felt her chest heave, and without intending it, she slapped her palm over her heart. "I lost my daughter, ten years ago."

Why had she said that? she wondered. To a complete stranger. What had that to do with this woman's recent loss? Now the tears would come; now she would have a meltdown before she ever had a chance to say what needed to be said. And what was it that needed saying? She had known for a while there, but she couldn't remember now to save herself. She wanted to turn and run back to the stupid Roto Rooter van and have herself a good cry. "I was in the car your son hit. Driving it. He hit me." She shook her head, disgusted with herself. "Though of course, he didn't mean—"

A hand appeared on the door frame, and all at once the chain fell away. The woman with the walker backed away, and a girl of fifteen or sixteen slid in front of her. "What do you want?" she snapped.

"I wanted to speak to Mrs. Hernandez."

The girl had a plain round face, pale lips, a birthmark, a mole, right along her whisper of a smile line. Her dark hair was long, parted on the side and pulled back into a ponytail. She was wearing jeans and a yellow t-shirt that said *Flash*. The potency of the message was diluted by the fact that the shirt was frayed at the neckline and several sizes too large on her. "She has no idea what you're saying. She doesn't speak English," she said. She lifted her arm and dropped it, a gesture of impatience. "She's not well either. She really doesn't want to be reminded about what happened."

It took Lola a moment to find her voice. "Are you … are you her caretaker?"

The arm again, raised and dropped. "I'm her granddaughter."

Lola's hand was back on her heart. Her eyes began watering. "You're his daughter?" Her voice broke, squeaking almost comically. None of the reports had said anything about a kid.

The arm, a third time. Lola couldn't help but be drawn to it. The girl wore a bracelet, a silver charm bracelet. Lola had had one too, back in her school days. So had Janet. Back then girls competed to see who could collect the most charms, because each charm told a story about you, about who you were and what you liked. Now kids had Instagram and Tiktok to share their stories. As far as Lola knew, charm bracelets were seriously passé. She wished she could get a better look at the one the girl was wearing. It only had two or three charms. Lola was curious to see what they were, what they might say about her. "Yes, Jamie Hernandez is my father," she said. "Was," she corrected. She lifted her chin, indignant.

Lola had to force herself to respond. "I wanted to know about him."

"You don't watch the news, lady?"

"No, I mean, yes, I know the story. I know what happened. I was there. But I want to know about *him*, what kind of man he was." That had come out wrong. He was an ex-felon. "I want to know what he loved in his life."

The girl turned, but not before Lola noticed her rolling her eyes. The woman, her grandmother, was saying something to her. She turned back to Lola. "Wait a minute," she said. The girl and her grandmother spoke back and forth, in Spanish. Lola glanced back, surprised all over again when she saw the van waiting for her, a big white elephant in the narrow driveway. When she turned around, the girl was looking at her. "Nana says not today. She doesn't feel up to visitors. But she says you can come back if you want."

"When?" Lola was suddenly excited.

The girl asked her grandmother. "Sunday, she says, after church."

"Church?"

The girl offered her a weak smile. She seemed nicer now. Or at least she didn't seem as irritated. Her arm had stopped flying out. Lola assumed the grandmother had said something about her attitude, chastened her maybe. "See you Sunday then."

Lola was already thinking that she could bring Pete with her. Or maybe Blue. She was imagining running that by Janet. Now that Janet had called George and told him not to come, she was happy with her old friend again. But regarding bringing the dogs over to the Hernandez house, she already knew what Janet would say. She would say it was entirely inappropriate. She was already hearing herself responding, "But the girl," and Janet listing all the reasons: The people could be dog haters; did she see any dogs there? No! They could have allergies; they could have cats. Janet, Lola conceded, would be right, this time. But she still couldn't keep the vision from playing in her head—the girl smiling, bending to pet both dogs, Jamie's daughter laughing, maybe, forgetting for a moment that her father was dead and she'd have to find a way to go on without him.

The girl and the grandmother stood at the door and watched her leave. She felt as if she was walking on rocks, or as if her legs were different lengths. Finally she reached her car, her van. She looked over her shoulder in time to see the door close.

On the way home Lola thought about Valerie's wake, a scenario that was always right there, a dark shadow from the past that fell over any number of activities performed in the present. She thought about how shocking it had been to see so many young people pouring in for those two days. The funeral home had had to open a partition wall between what had been two reception rooms to make one big one. *Good thing we only had the one body*, she'd heard the funeral director's assistant say to the director. Lola remembered thinking—cruelly, she knew, but she couldn't help it—that if all these kids who were coming in clutching one another, sobbing their little hearts out, had been kinder to Valerie when she was living, maybe she still would be. She remembered thinking that the kids had likely come not so much because they had cared about Valerie—she wondered how many had even known her—but because young people didn't know anything about death at that age. Valerie's passing was their chance to explore it from a safe distance, to learn how it worked, what it looked like, how it impacted the life around it. A chance to get close to it. Fifteen- and sixteen- and seventeen-year-olds were undergoing change constantly— change of classes, of class*rooms*, of partners, of friends, changes in their own bodies. The permanence of death, the irreversibility of it, was unacceptable, but also an allurement—isolated and irresistible, a magnetic force.

All those children filing past, an endless stream of them, nodding their condolences when they reached Lola and George. Very few stopped to actually say anything more than *sorry* to them. But there was one girl—wide-eyed, wringing her hands, frantic looking. She was taller than the other girls, taller than some of the boys, and she tried to hide it by slouching, her thick auburn hair draped over half her face. Lola found herself wanting to say, *Honey, stand up straight; people will always be too busy noticing your bad posture, making assumptions about how you feel about yourself, to see how beautiful you are,* though of course she would never have done such a thing under any circumstances. Because she knew it would backfire, make the child even more self-conscious. Lola herself was taller than she'd ever wanted to be. She was nearly thirty when she managed to stop slouching. When the girl reached Lola, she surprised her by stepping in close, whispering in her ear. "I saw her yesterday," she said, turning back at once to see if the person behind her might have heard. But the line was snaking around her and Lola, going directly to

George, who was trying to smile and be good-natured. "She was wearing a blue robe," the girl continued.

Lola grabbed the girl's hand. Later she would wonder just how tightly she had held it; later she would imagine that she might have hurt the girl. At the very least she must have scared her, clutching at her like that. No one could have known Valerie's robe was blue. Even when she went on her so-called sleepovers, she left the robe behind.

"She was moving around, looking at things, like she'd lost something, or like she didn't know where she was. I was scared, seeing her, you know? I wanted to go to her and ask if I could help. But I knew I wasn't supposed to be seeing her and so ..." The girl began to cry. She looked behind her again. So many people. An army of adolescents. She squeezed her fingers out of Lola's grasp. "I thought you'd want to know," she said. She waited a beat for a response, but Lola was speechless, and so she moved off.

Amanda, Lola would eventually remember her name was. She'd seen her at awards ceremonies, reluctantly climbing the stairs at the side of the stage to accept one certificate of honor after another. A level-headed girl, an A student hiding behind all that hair and bad posture; not a crackpot. If Valerie had visited Amanda, a girl who was not even part of her small social circle as far as Lola knew, didn't that mean she might visit Lola one day too?

Usually Lola hated that Janet knew every little thing going on in her life, but ever since she'd laid down the law a few days back and told Janet to call George and tell him not to come, she felt a new respect for her old friend. Janet had gone right home that day, made the call, and come back across the street to report it. The dogs must have been expecting her, because they never even barked. Janet had walked right in and through the house and knocked on Lola's bedroom door. But before Lola, who was still thinking about the hawk that Valerie had encountered, could decide whether or not to answer, she called out, "Mission accomplished. I told him it's not a good time. I'm going home now." And she did. She left. And Lola didn't see her at all the next day, which was something of a relief. It gave Lola the time she needed to clear her head, to make decisions about both buying the van *and* going to visit Jamie's mother so that she might learn something about the man whose death was now inextricably bound to her life. And it went the other way too. Like Amanda, who had brought her a kind of knotted hope, maybe there was something Lola could say or do that would give Jamie's mother—and now his daughter as well—some small comfort, though she couldn't imagine what it might be.

Lola saw Janet go out the day before and return a while later with a bag of groceries. Ordinarily she would have driven right into her garage, but she must have been planning to go out again because she parked in front of her house and went in through the front gate. Usually Janet called ahead to see if Lola wanted anything from the store. Lola never did—or even if she did, she always said she didn't. She resented Janet for asking, and then she always felt guilty if *she* didn't ask when *she* went to the store. She resented the intimacy the gesture implied. It was as if they were back in junior high again, running back and forth across the street to borrow a scarf or a belt to complete an outfit so they could look their best at a football game or at parties in the park with the other neighborhood kids.

Lola was thinking all this too as she drove home from the Hernandez place. She was admonishing herself for being so resistant to Janet's friendship all these years. She'd always wanted a sister when she was a kid—and here she had one, sort of, and she didn't appreciate it. She should have been ecstatic to have Janet in her life, someone to know and care whether she lived or died. There were times she was so lonely. So, *so* lonely. What was wrong with her? Why was she always pushing back on the one constant she had: Janet's friendship, Janet's attentiveness?

As soon as she got home, she decided, she was going to march across the street and tell Janet she'd been to the Hernandez house, that Jamie Hernandez had a daughter, that the girl had a charm bracelet just like the ones the two of them had had as kids, that she'd been invited to come back to the house on Sunday, that she might or might not bring Pete along. Or Blue. She would flood Janet with the only thing she really ever wanted from Lola—privileged information, secrets, intimacy. She was going to open her heart for once and let Janet walk on in—years' worth of mountains of baggage and all—because that was what friends did. That's what *sisters* did. And the next time Janet called to ask if she needed anything from the store, she was going to say yes, yes indeed, even if she had to make something up. Or maybe she'd suggest they go together.

But as she was turning into her driveway, she saw that Janet had company. There was a new-looking white sedan parked out in front of her adobe wall. She had nearly completed the turn when she realized that Janet's gate was wide open, and Janet and her visitor were sitting on a bench on the patio, under the desert willow tree. Who could it be?

She couldn't say. She'd only caught a glimpse. She parked the van along the side of her house, between it and her shop, and looked in the sideview mirror. Janet and her companion—it was a man—weren't talking at the moment, but they must have been, because their torsos were angled toward each other, their knees almost touching. They seemed to be watching her watching them. She got out of the car and turned to face them. The man half rose and removed his sunglasses. It couldn't be. But it was.

George.

6

BEN

know yourself

Ben was nearly back to the ledge when he saw Vince's head pop up over the rail above the overpass. Then he was right there, at Ben's side, saying, "Let me help, buddy." He took Ben's sleeping bag and trash bag and started heading back with them. Ben was wondering where all this goodwill had sprung from when he reached the ledge himself and Derrick, who was squatting near his plastic owl, shouted, "Vince won. We're rich!"

Vince dropped Ben's stuff at once and monkey-jumped his way to Derrick and put his hands around his throat. "What'd I tell you? I told you never—"

Derrick opened his eyes wide, then squeezed them shut. His features scrunched; he was about to cry. But he must have realized he was in the right this time, for all at once he straightened and his features sprang back in place. "No," he shouted in Vince's face. "You said no one *but* Ben. You said Ben could know 'cause he's part of it. Remember, Vince?"

Vince thought about that. Slowly he relaxed his grip on Derrick's neck, then let go altogether. When he looked back at Ben, Ben could see that his face had gone red, maybe with shame. *Humph*, he grunted under his breath; he had never thought of Vince as someone capable of experiencing shame. Or maybe what he saw on Vince's face was simply the residue of his anger. He carefully placed Siggy's carrier against the wall of the ledge, where no one would accidentally trip on it. "You won money?" he asked cautiously.

Vince reached in his shirt pocket and pulled out a pack of filter-less Camels and a yellow disposable lighter. Usually when he reached into his pocket it was to produce a butt he'd picked up on the street. He smirked while he lit up. "My cousin," he said out of the side of his mouth. "He loaned me money to bet the horses, 'cause I got horse sense and he don't. Said we'd split if I won." He shrugged. "I won. Just one race. But it was a good win, a once in a blue moon win." He blew smoke through a wide grin.

Ben didn't know what to say. "So, you leaving us? You going back to live in the white man's world?" He chuckled.

"No, man. It ain't *that* kind of money. Five hundred bucks, give or take. That ain't going to change my life unless I grow it."

"Yeah, grow it," Derrick cried. He rubbed his palms together gleefully.

"So, what? You're planning on planting it out in the field, in one of the squirrel holes?"

"Yeah," Vince said sarcastically. "And we're all going to take turns pissing on it until it turns into a money tree."

Derrick liked that. He tossed his head back and laughed raucously. Both men stared at him a moment. Then Ben said, "Okay, a money tree. I'll piss on it; I'll do my part, sure. For a minute I thought we were going to bring it down to the Morgan Stanley and buy some stocks."

"You're not far off," Vince said, smirking again.

Ben studied him. He was getting nervous now. He didn't want to be connected to any of Vince's schemes.

Vince perched himself on the edge of the ledge and slapped his palm on the space beside him. Ben looked back at the carrier then sat down carefully, conscious of his clean jeans. "So," Vince began, "I got this friend, Sam Brite, his name is, who has a casino card for Sandia. He says if I give him ten bucks, I can borrow the card tonight, along with his I.D., which means I get a room in the hotel for his discounted price—a really good one because he's there all the time giving the Injuns his hard-earned cash. Between the room and the money I have to give him, I'm down one bill and four to go. You following so far?"

Ben nodded. He glanced over his shoulder at the carrier again.

"So, me and you, we split the four and play the tables. We lose, well, so what? It was gravy to begin with. You understand? And it bought us a night off the ledge. But if we win … If we win … I tell ya, I'm feeling so damn lucky right now, man." He closed his eyes and shook his head, marveling. Then he cleared his throat and turned his head to the side and spit. He took a deep drag from his cigarette. "We win, we split it, seventy-five/twenty-five. 'Cause it's my money. It's my lucky streak we'll be riding." As if Ben had confronted him, he thumbed his chest, hard. Then he flicked what was left of his cigarette. It flew out over the bike path below them, over the edge and down the steep slope into the arroyo, where it was carried along with other debris in the small stream heading for the Rio Grande.

Ben looked up from its passage to see Vince staring at him, grinning ear to ear. He was a handsome young dude; Ben had never noticed before. His teeth were straight and fairly white, considering how much he smoked. His brows were straight. He had a strong nose, and even a dimple at one side of his mouth. "Let me ask you," Ben began. "You're a smart young guy. How'd you wind up living under a bridge?"

"You in or not, old man?"

Ben thought about how he had taken a shower the night before. He'd charged his phone; he'd had a good night's sleep; he was wearing clean jeans and a clean t-shirt, and he had a clean button-down ready to change into at the top of his trash bag. It should have been an easy decision. But the truth was, he liked gambling. Or he had, back in the days when he had a little extra money now and then. He'd won a few poker hands over the years, once walking out with two grand more than he'd walked in with. That was a night to remember. He'd used the money to take Ruthie skiing for the weekend, up in Red River. They'd stayed in a lodge with a spa, and both evenings Ruthie ended her day on the trails with a soak in one of the hot tubs and a hot stone massage. Sometimes she'd gone to the casino along with him. She liked to play the slots. She said it distracted her from the mess the world was in.

"Come on, man," Vince said. His pleasant smile was gone now. His lips thinned when he pressed them together. His brows seemed too close to his eyes. "I can't do it without you."

"Sure you can," Ben said. "And think of this. If you do it alone, you won't have to split it." He almost added that if it was companionship Vince needed, he could take Derrick along. But he figured Vince would make some crack about Derrick being stupid, so he kept his mouth shut.

Vince turned his head to the side and shook it. "Ain't gonna work without you, man. Might as well burn the lettuce and forget about ever getting out of the soup."

Derrick's shrill laughter again, but Vince shut it down with one quick glance. "I don't get it," Ben said. "Since when did you get so needy, tough guy? I thought you had horse sense."

"I ain't needy, old man," Vince snapped. He opened his mouth, closed it, opened it again. "I *know* horses, like the back of my hand. I don't know the games. I don't know the tables. You do. You said back in the old days, you had some luck, burned the house down one night."

Ben didn't remember ever having had such a conversation with Vince. "I told you that?" he asked.

Vince stuck his index finger to the side of his head. "Duh! I pay attention, man. I got a brain like a fucking elephant. You didn't tell me; you told that blond dame you brought here that time. The one whose husband offed himself. It wasn't meant for my ears, but I heard it anyway and I stored it." He let his hand drop. "Because I had a feeling it would be useful one day. All information becomes useful if you wait long enough."

Ben remembered now. He and Nancy had been talking about luck, about serendipity, how sometimes it seemed like forces outside yourself were dropping crumbs, tempting you to follow. How we all wanted to believe in a trustworthy world, one that offered guidance if we took the time to look for it, but sometimes you got fooled; you got played by the forces that be. He laughed. "Where you from, anyway?" he asked. He was buying time. Gambling, especially with someone else's money, was not a good idea. But then again, it wasn't illegal. He was waiting for the voice in his head that was enthusiastically trying to convince him to acquiesce to run out of steam and shut itself down.

Vince stared at him for a half a minute before answering. "Bangor."

"Bangor?" Ben began to laugh. "Bangor, Maine?" He could hear Derrick starting up behind him, but he didn't look at him. "Stephen King territory? You ever see King walking around up there? With his dogs? He likes corgis, right? I read that somewhere." He did not believe Vince for a New York minute. He was no more from Bangor than Ben was. "That where you learned so much about horses, up in Bangor?" he added, still laughing.

"Listen, man," Vince said, his face darkening. "You don't want to come, that's fine. You don't want a clean room and a hot shower, a chance to split some bucks should we be so lucky, that's all fine and good by me. Just forget I ever said—"

Ben interrupted with a bark of indignation. "Calm down there, young fellow. I'm just a little surprised to hear you're from Bangor. That's all. I never would have guessed it. *Ayuh?* Look, I have some stuff I need to do today, calls I need to make. I got my phone charged and ready to go. Does it have to be tonight?"

"Tonight's the night, with or without you. And think of this, Mr. Old Man Smartass. You stay in a nice hotel room tonight, your phone will be charged fresh again tomorrow anyway."

Ben thought about that. It would mean another good night's sleep, another shower. All he'd be doing is putting off his search for work by one day. "And what about Siggy? What am I supposed to do with him?"

Vince cocked his head in Derrick's direction. Immediately Derrick's hand flew up from where it had been resting atop Owl's head.

"Derrick doesn't like to stay alone on the ledge at night. You know that."

"He won't be alone. He'll have Mr. Plastic Owl to watch out for him. *And* kitty cat. That ain't alone in my book."

"Come on, Vince. Don't be a jerk. He can't stay alone."

Vince shrugged. "Then we drag his fat ass with us, him and the cat. We all sleep in one room. Cat would like that. He'll get to stretch his legs in a nice clean room for once."

Ben got up slowly and monkey-walked the distance between his section of the ledge and the section that was Derrick's. Derrick watched him coming, his mouth open, the tip of his tongue tapping against his upper lip rhythmically. "You good with that?" he asked. Derrick nodded.

Ben turned to Vince, who was up too now, bent in half, gazing down at the arroyo. "Okay," he said at last. "When do we leave? And what's the plan for getting there?"

"Give me your phone," Vince said. "I got to call my friend, Sam Brite."

He handed Vince the phone. "Passcode is—"

"Yeah, yeah, I know what it is."

7

LOLA

the dance

Lola dashed into the side entrance and locked the door behind her. Then she ran into the living room and peeked through the front window. She was sure it was George, but she needed another look. She wanted to be one hundred percent certain before she called Janet and told her she never wanted to speak to her again, *ever*, for as long as she lived.

But what was this? Janet was scurrying across the street, her short legs moving beneath her like two balls of tumbleweed in a stiff wind, her hand clutching the ends of her hand-woven cashmere shawl to keep it from flying away. She'd closed her patio gate behind her. Presumably George was still sitting there behind it. At least Lola hoped that was the case. As soon as Janet was close enough, Lola threw the door open and shouted, "You told me you told him not to come."

"I did! I said don't come, and he came anyway! What was I supposed to do?"

Lola glanced across the street. She didn't want to be caught standing there with the door wide open with George in such close proximity. If he opened the gate and looked, he might mistake it for an invitation. But she couldn't bring herself to slam the door in Janet's face either. "How did he even know your address?"

"I gave it to him, when I told him to come, before I told him not to. He would have figured it out anyway, Lola. Everything's on the internet. Everything is knowable. Welcome to the twenty-first century."

"Get in," Lola snapped, standing back. Once Janet was inside, Lola reached behind her to close and lock the door. Then she marched into the kitchen, Janet on her heels, and threw herself down on a chair. "I. Do. Not. Want. To. See. Him," she declared. "Please explain that to him and make him go away. Or, if you can't manage that, then keep him at your house. Whatever. I don't care, as long as he doesn't come here."

"Lola, listen to yourself!" Janet cried. Both dogs had followed them into the kitchen and were staring at her, alert. She lowered her voice. "He came all this way. He drove. From Miami. You know how many miles that is?"

"No. Do you?"

Janet approached Lola's chair, but Lola swung herself sideways, stubbornly facing the sink. "Lola, how is this loving the Earth and everything that lives on it?" Janet asked, her voice an octave lower than usual. "That's what I want to know."

Lola was so steaming angry that at first she didn't catch the reference. When she did, she tossed her head back and rolled her eyes to the ceiling. She'd written some poems the previous year. A local publisher who was a friend of hers had published them in chapbook format. She didn't really consider herself a poet; she'd simply felt compelled to express her views about climate crisis, about the fact that Earth was in extinction mode, with its flora and fauna disappearing at a thousand times the historical rate. If it was true that we were past the tipping point—and scientists seemed to agree that was the case—and climate crisis was only going to get worse, leaving more and more people homeless and starving, then our job was to love the Earth more than ever, to infuse it with love, to love it madly, every blade of grass, every leaf on every tree, not because an infusion of love might reverse things—though Lola secretly believed that was a possibility—but because Earth was beautiful and wonderful, a mother to all of us, and we had collectively failed to appreciate her, and this was our last chance to make up for it, to adore her, to ride out on tide of gratitude, for Earth and for one another, for all sentient creatures. A handful of people had showed up for her reading at a local independent bookstore, Janet of course being one of them.

"Loving the Earth has nothing to do with opening myself up for abuse," Lola cried. She resented Janet even more for trying to use her own dumb poems against her.

But Janet seemed determined to fuel her resentment. She spread her arms dramatically, even though Lola was turned aside and could only see her peripherally. "Oh, we must fall to our knees and love our planet mother," Janet cried loudly, maliciously. "We must love every single insect, every fucking rodent." (Lola turned her head to give her a quick look; Janet hardly ever cursed.) "We must get all up in arms because a poisonous frog that lives in Costa Rica is on his deathbed," Janet continued. "And a white rhinoceros, for God's sake! I know I'm going to miss seeing *him* on the planet! And what about the snouted cobra? Most people would say his passing was a good thing, one less snake to have to worry about. But not you. And trash! I almost forgot trash! It's not enough to clean up our own but we must pick up other people's too. And of course we must avoid plastic at all costs. Things come and go, Lola. That's life."

Lola shook her head. Janet was a madwoman. None of the poems said anything like that. The snouted cobra wasn't even extinct yet, as far as she knew. And certainly Lola had not sounded like a pompous ass when she'd read the couple of poems that were about the species that *were* extinct.

"Oh, we must love one another, forgive one another," Janet went on. "We must open our hearts like never before. And why? Because the end of times is upon us."

Lola's whisper cut through the air between them like a blade. "You're crazy, Janet," she said. "You're ignorant. You know where the word ignorant comes from? *Ignore.* You see what I see but you ignore it because it's inconvenient. That's what the poems are about, opening your eyes, seeing what's going on and choosing *not* to ignore it. You didn't even know that, did you?"

She liked to think her poems were Whitman-esque, a breathless brimming, throbbing listing of all the things there were to know and love on the planet. The wonderment of living in such a place. But if this was Janet's takeaway, then maybe she'd gotten it wrong. Maybe she'd written doggerel. Except to say *that was nice* as they were leaving, Janet had never commented on the poems in her chapbook or her reading before. Lola hadn't realized she'd even paid attention. She'd figured she'd slept through it, like she slept through everything else that didn't impact her directly.

Janet went around the table and pulled out the chair closest to Lola. "Yes I did. You said we should think of the dying Earth as we would a dying loved one. If we knew our loved one was on her way out, we would want to be with her every last minute, give her all the love we had so that when she passes, we know we made her last days the best we could."

Lola scoffed. "The Earth's not going anywhere, Janet. We made the planet sick, but once we're gone, she'll recover very quickly. Look how quickly she started to recover during COVID, when everyone was on lockdown." She dropped her head and mumbled to herself, "Unless there's a nuclear holocaust. Then it might take a little longer."

"Yada yada yada. Wars and hatred. Dictatorships and pandemics. What's it matter who's dying, us or the planet? I don't really care what happens to Mother Earth if we're all going up in smoke anyway."

Lola gasped. She couldn't believe Janet had just said that.

Janet got up as suddenly as she'd sat down. "You're such a hypocrite, Lola. *Love love love.* You pretend to be a fifty-seven-year-old flower child. But who the hell do *you* love? Dogs. That's who. Drooling, barking, food-centric dogs."

Janet glanced at Pete and Blue, who had gotten bored with the argument but were still attending it, now lying side by side on the kitchen floor, their heads resting on criss-crossed paws, their eyes on her. "And people who like dogs. Oh yeah, and tatted-up people who broadside you and then threaten the life of some poor woman down the street. And all those homeless people who you think saved your life after your incident. Yada yada yada yada. I'm so sick of hearing it all. But your ex-husband, poor soul who regrets that he cheated on you *ONE WHOLE TIME … All* my husbands cheated on me, Lola, and *way* more than once! No, for him, for George, you can't find even a little grain-of-sand-sized fleck of forgiveness. And don't ever talk to me again about how having a nice juicy steak every now and then is being complicit in the demise of the rain forest—heck, in the end of the world!—because that's pure bullshit coming from a hypocrite like you. You lack hope, Lola. That's your problem. Things can change, but you'll be blinded by your cynicism and you'll never even notice."

Someone knocked. The dogs had been so engaged in Janet's theatrical monologue that it took them a few seconds to orient themselves and react. They jumped to attention in unison and raced to the door, barking furiously. Lola took a breath and closed her eyes. "I'm letting him in," Janet declared loudly as she left the room.

"Don't let him in. I'll never forgive you."

"Don't forgive me. I don't give a shit anymore."

All at once Lola felt tired, tired and weak. Drained. She longed for this day to be over. Or at least this moment, the unfolding situation it encompassed.

She heard Janet in the living room, calming the dogs. They must have thought Janet was authorized to act as Lola's surrogate because they actually listened to her and fell silent. She heard the door creaking open. She heard George and Janet whispering, rather urgently, she thought. She heard George nervously saying hello to the dogs, remarking to Janet about Pete's size, asking if he was aggressive. She heard his footsteps approaching, *tap slide tap slide tap slide,* on the Saltillo tiles. She turned back toward the table and stretched one arm out on it, and then dropped her head on her arm, facing in the direction from which George would soon appear.

And then he was there, George, his hair gone gray and somewhat thinner, but still curly, and a neatly trimmed pepper-colored beard to match. He looked like a sea captain, like Sir Thomas Lipton with a perm, and without the bulk.

His posture was off somehow. Lola remembered that his hip had been bothering him the last time she'd seen him. Apparently it had gotten worse. He stretched one arm to take hold of the back of the nearest chair, perhaps for balance. "Hello, Lola," he said.

"Hello, George." She forced herself to lift her head, to straighten. She forced her lips to turn up at the corners. "Cup of coffee? Maybe some cookies?"

"I'd love some coffee. No cookies, thank you."

"You sure? They're homemade banana oatmeal." Actually the neighbor, Mrs. Quick, had made them, more than a week ago. Lola hadn't eaten any because Mrs. Quick had topped them with that same strange-looking blackish-greenish gummy thing as last time, the thing Janet had said looked like bird shit. They were probably stale by now.

"No, thank you," he said again. Lola looked beyond him. George turned too and then back. "Janet?" he asked. "She went back to her house after she let me in," he said.

"*Humph*," Lola grunted, pushing herself to her feet.

He pulled out the chair he'd been holding on to and lowered himself gingerly.

"So how's Florida?" Lola asked, turning her back to him. She poured two mugs from the pot and stuck them in the microwave.

"Nice. A little too warm this time of year."

"Um-hum."

For the next ninety-five seconds she watched the tray rotate through the glass window of the microwave. When the appliance pinged, she opened the door and removed the mugs and set them on the table. "Cream or sugar, George?" she asked, though she knew he didn't take either.

"No, thank you."

Finally she sat.

"Look, I'm sorry for barging in like this," he said, his head tilted downward and at an angle.

She shook her head. "It's just that it's unnecessary, George. I was in an accident, as you know—from Janet's Facebook I've been made to understand—but I walked away without a scratch. I'm perfectly fine, as you can see. She must have told you."

"Yes, she told me you were fine. I didn't come because I thought you were injured. I came because …"

He looked down at the table, then into his cup. Pete stepped into the kitchen to slurp from his water bowl. George watched him. For all that Pete was otherwise perfect, he was a loud and sloppy drinker, and he left a puddle of water behind and walked away slobbering. When he was back in the other room, George finally looked at Lola. "I'm sorry," he said. "I came to say I'm very sorry that I ruined our marriage." He took a deep breath and exhaled slowly.

Lola scoffed. "That was what? Nine years ago now, George? Nine years after the fact and you decide to drop in from two thousand miles away and apologize?" She was pleased to hear how level her voice was, almost monotone, barely above a whisper.

He had no immediate answer, so Lola calmly continued. "Your friend Janet likes to remind me that it was only the one time that you cheated on me." She laughed joylessly. "But it was your timing, George. I'm not going to get into it with you now, nine years after the fact, but you spent a weekend with a woman you'd only just met while I was so deep in grief I couldn't see straight, while—"

"And did you think I wasn't grieving myself?" George interrupted. "We lost our daughter. I was lost. I was blind with grief. I lost my way. Grief was all around me. It was suffocating me—your grief, my grief." His voice was low too, almost instructional. "That's the way it happens. For men at least. Not all men, I guess. I shouldn't have said that. But one day I was myself and the next day I was someone else. I was a stranger. A stranger who thought he'd found a temporary fix for his merciless pain. Valerie was gone and you were gone and I made a colossal mistake, and you couldn't get over it. Not that I'm blaming you. Never. I'm just trying to say what happened, from my perspective."

Lola shook her head. She couldn't believe they were having this conversation, nine years later. She wanted to end it, but somehow she found herself diving in again. "A whole weekend! With someone you'd only just met. At a post-production party in Santa Fe, not the kind of thing most men would have even attended, having just lost their child days before. But off you went, and then the two of you, flying to New Orleans for a three-day weekend. Music and French Quarter restaurants. It was all a bit over the top." Lola was amazed to realize how front of mind the details were, after all this time.

"It doesn't matter who or how or where. I hardly knew what I was doing. It felt inevitable. It felt lifesaving at the time. It was a distraction. From myself. A stupid one. But then I couldn't take it back. I couldn't erase it. It was too big a hurdle. I knew we would never get beyond it."

"And so you left. Instead of trying to work it out, you left."

He lowered his head. "Yes. I left. You know you would never have forgiven me. I knew I was never going to forgive myself."

Lola nodded. She sipped her coffee. George had been her boyfriend in high school, for three or four dizzying months. He was very popular back then, and considered to be one of the best-looking boys in their grade. Football quarterback. Debate team. A boy who loved to laugh. Always, girls were chasing him. She didn't expect their relationship to last. They were only sixteen after all. And she was quiet and shy, and self-conscious about her height. It was only a matter of time, she was certain, until he figured out that there were plenty of other girls who would make for a better fit.

They never actually *broke up*. You didn't have to in those days. One day he approached her in the hall, after the last bell. When he reached her, he put his hands on her shoulders and looked into her eyes for a few long moments and then bent his head so as to be able to lean his forehead against hers. "You're so sweet," he'd whispered. Three words. One at a time. *You're. So. Sweet.* The next day she saw him walking hand-in-hand in the hall with Flower Jackson, a beautiful, vivacious girl, a more suitable counterpart, the both of them laughing. She wasn't surprised. But she knew she would miss him. A lot.

She started dating a physics major her first year in college, Dennis. He'd wanted to become an astrophysicist, but he didn't want to teach his way through masters and doctorate programs to get there. In a perfect world, he would have found an internship in a space lab. What he took instead was a great-paying job as a research assistant for a wealth management company out in Columbus. He said he hated it.

He and Lola were living in a small fourth-floor walkup in Springfield by then. Lola had a degree in Animal Shelter Management and she had a job investigating and writing and speaking at conferences on various related topics. She loved her work. It required her to meet with other professionals in the animal sciences to discuss things like animal nutrition, reproduction, genetics, etc.

Her office was in downtown Springfield and she seldom left the area, but one day she got a call from a woman—her name was Ginger—who said she was about to graduate from the American Institute of Alternative Medicine in Columbus. Ginger already had an undergraduate degree in zoology, and she was hoping Lola might have some good ideas about where she could find work that would combine her two interests. Lola didn't think it would be much of a problem; a lot of clinical research centers were already in place working toward the same purpose. She could have given her a list of the ones she was familiar with over the phone, but Ginger, who lived in Columbus, asked if they could meet for lunch. She said she'd read several of Lola's white papers and really wanted to meet her in person. Her treat. She had a great restaurant in mind, there in Columbus. Lola, who was as susceptible to flattery as anyone, agreed.

Ginger suggested they meet at Buckley's, a high-end seafood place located in a high-end mall. Even though it was early spring and not very cold anymore, Ginger said she would wear a bright red scarf, so that Lola would be able to identify her. Lola said she would wear a dark blue scarf. They agreed to meet near the restaurant entrance.

Lola found a place to park in the crowded lot and located Buckley's on the mall directory map and was headed in that direction when a woman in a bright red scarf walking ahead of her caught her eye. She would have called out, but it couldn't have been Ginger, because the woman was walking hand-in-hand with a man, a man in a suit, a man who looked like Dennis from the back. But it couldn't have been Dennis because everyone in his office ordered in, every day, because they had so much work. That was one of the things he always complained about.

She spotted Buckley's coming up ahead, on the left. The woman in the red scarf and the man who looked like Dennis from the back seemed to be headed there too. When they turned to enter, Lola, who had stopped walking to watch them, got a good look at both of them. They were stunning together, with their thick dark hair and blue eyes, both laughing. Before they disappeared, the woman turned and looked right at her. She flashed a big smile, all white teeth and pink gums.

That night Lola questioned Dennis. She didn't say she was in Columbus and had seen him in the mall. She just asked what he'd had for lunch. He was reading a magazine. He didn't look up. Chinese, he said. The whole office ordered in, Chinese.

In the morning Lola called in sick and then called a realtor, and together they found an affordable studio that Lola could move into right away. She stopped at a supermarket on the way back for boxes and packed up her books and clothes and some personal items. Then she walked down the street to the local YMCA and offered two young men who had just left the facility and were heading for their car a hundred dollars to help her move her stuff. She was out of the walkup and settled into the studio before Dennis was even due home from work.

A few days later, she was shopping in her new neighborhood's deli when she bumped into George, whom she hadn't seen in almost eight years. His mouth dropped open when he recognized her. She couldn't really cook anything yet because she had left all the pots and pans behind with Dennis, taking only one place setting and two water glasses for herself. Accordingly, she was carrying a baguette, a package of Asiago, a container of grilled vegetables, and carton of blackberries. George had a bottle of red wine, a container of black bean soup, and another of mixed olives. They looked at each other's stash and laughed. "Wow," George said. "If we put your stuff and my stuff together, we could have an amazing dinner." He cocked his head. "You free to do that?"

"Yes," Lola replied gleefully. All she could think was, if not for Ginger, she'd still be with Dennis, and she'd have said, *No, I'm not free, though I really wish I were.* Or probably, because she was who she was, she would have just said, *No, I'm not free, though I appreciate the offer.* Of course if not for Ginger she would have missed the invitation altogether, because she wouldn't have been in the new neighborhood.

Years later when people asked how they'd gotten together, Lola would say they were high school sweethearts, but that wasn't true and she'd have to correct herself. Finally George told her not to bother, that the time between their fling in high school and their reunion in the deli didn't count as far as he was concerned. Serendipity; every day she believed that, right up until the unthinkable happened.

So yes, she had turned away from George in her moment of grief, but she always planned to turn back. But then he spent the weekend with another woman, a stranger.

"And so, why are you here, exactly?" she asked now, a trace of unintended heat in her tone. "I mean, I'm glad we've cleared the air, but why are we having this conversation now?"

George, who had been about to lift his mug to his lips, set it back down. He cleared his throat. He shrugged. "I'm dying, Lola."

"What?" The word came out sounding like a gust of wind.

"I probably have three or four months to go. I can never forgive myself for what I did to you, to us. But I'm hoping that you'll forgive me at some point, for your sake, because mine won't matter once I'm gone. I don't think. Who knows for sure?" He smiled his slightly lopsided smile and shrugged. "But be that as it may, I don't want you to have to carry the burden of …" He fizzled out.

Lola was speechless. She turned her head to the side, toward the sink, blinking, her mouth slightly agape.

George slapped his hands on his thighs and got up slowly. "And so that's that. That's what I came to say. Even if you can't forgive me just yet, maybe you'll think better of me at some point in the future. You were the one true love of my life. You *were* my life." He glanced toward the living room. Both dogs were watching him from the sofa. "I'm leaving now, Lola. I'm going to hit the road as soon as I freshen up at Janet's. I have a doctor's appointment to get back for. Thank you for seeing me."

He walked out of the room, out of the house.

Lola could feel the world brimming and throbbing all around her.

8

BEN

synchronicity

They got a standard queen. The king would have been slightly less money, but the queen had two beds. As soon as they walked in the room and Ben saw the longing with which Derrick was staring at the bed nearest the bathroom, he told him he could have it; Ben would sleep on the floor. Derrick reacted by jumping three inches into the air and then throwing himself hard on the bed. As Ben turned to have a look at the bathroom, he heard Vince tell Derrick to knock it off, but he said it softly, and it didn't come off as offensive as usual.

The bathroom was to die for; that's how Ruthie would have put it. It was huge and had a long deep soaking tub, big enough for a man to float in. "First dibs on the tub," Ben announced over his shoulder.

Vince popped his head into the room immediately. "Wait a minute," he warned, eyeing the tub. "This is my gig, my—"

"True enough," Ben said. "But I had a shower yesterday. The tub will still be clean when I climb out. Can you say the same?"

Vince snarled at him, but he could hardly argue. He jutted his chin at the oversized walk-in shower on the other side of the room. "I don't do baths anyway," he mumbled. "Baths are for girls and faggots."

Ben locked himself in, stripped down, turned the faucets on full blast and climbed in. He expected Vince to beat on the door at some point and complain that he was taking too long, but when he turned off the faucets he could hear that they had put the TV on. He heard gunfire and a lot of shouting. He imagined Vince and Derrick were mesmerized and had forgotten all about him, for the moment at least.

He soaked for nearly an hour, until there was no warmth left in the water at all. Back home, he had never taken baths. It had seemed a waste of time, time that could be spent mowing the lawn, raking the leaves, or doing any one of a number of minor (and sometimes not-so-minor) repairs around the house. He couldn't remember the last time he'd felt so relaxed, both physically—all the tension had gone out of his muscles; he felt like rubber—and mentally. The towel he wrapped himself in afterward was so soft and luxurious that he forgot for a moment that he was a homeless man who would be back to sleeping under an overpass in the middle of the city in no time.

Ben walked out of the bathroom and glanced at the TV. Men in cowboy hats and Clint Eastwood-style ponchos on horses: they were watching a Western. Vince was sitting at the end of his bed, his elbows on his knees, leaning over to be as close as possible to the screen. Derrick was already under the covers in his bed, in his filthy street clothes, his pillows punched up to support his head. Ben made a mental note to suggest he take a shower in the morning. He didn't figure Derrick would think to do so on his own.

Siggy was curled up against Derrick's side, purring close to his ear. They'd stopped to buy some sub sandwiches on the way to the resort, and the wrapper from Derrick's was open on the bedside table. "I fed him already," Derrick said when he noticed Ben looking his way. Ben had planned to feed Siggy himself, because he didn't want Derrick accidentally letting something spicy get into Siggy's bowl. Derrick must have read Ben's thoughts because he took his eyes off the screen again long enough to add, "He had ham and cheese. I rinsed it good so he wouldn't get dressing."

"What did you rinse it in?" Ben asked.

Derrick jerked his head sideways, a gesture he'd picked up from Vince—perfected now after so many hours in his company—toward the water pitcher and glass, also on the bedside table. Ben could see bits of lettuce and what looked like red-pepper flakes floating in the glass. He looked at Siggy, who was looking back at him, seemingly saying, *See? Derrick takes almost as good care of me as you do.* Ben wondered if Derrick missed his owl. He'd asked Vince if he could bring him along, and when Vince said no, he'd turned to Ben, his bottom lip protruding. "It'll be okay," Ben had reassured him. "He knows his job is to guard the place while we're away. Anyone wants to move onto the ledge, he'll scare them off. That's his job. Owls are protectors." Derrick had nodded reluctantly, but he held back a moment when Sam Brite called down to announce his arrival from the top of the overpass, to say a silent farewell, Ben surmised.

An hour later Ben and Vince were down in the casino, two good-looking men, clean men; they could have been father and son. When they'd first entered the gaming area, Ben had been wearing his sunglasses, just in case he ran into anyone he knew. Everyone from his previous life knew he was homeless. It would be embarrassing as hell to have to try to explain what he was doing in a casino. Not that anyone would dare to ask. But if someone saw him and told Ruthie, Ruthie would tell Moon and he'd never win her back. His baby girl. The stab of pain that came attached to his every thought about her always felt fresh. Vince picked up on his jitters and called him out, saying, "Relax, old man. Look around. Everyone's focused on winning." Ben looked. Vince was right. Everyone there had a mission. That was the one thing they all had in common. *Money won is twice as sweet as money earned*: Paul Newman, *The Color of Money*. He removed his sunglasses and stuck them in his shirt pocket.

They played a few slots as part of their warm-up strategy and walked away more or less even after a half hour. Then they went to the roulette table, where Ben bought fifty one-dollar chips, which, with a five-dollar-a-spin minimum, would buy them ten games. When he turned to give half to Vince, Vince took a giant step backwards. "What, are you afraid to place a bet?" Ben asked.

"You do it," Vince snapped, jutting his chin toward the number layout.

Ben stared at him for a beat. And then, because the croupier's hand was lifting, signaling that he was about to sweep it over the table and announce there'd be no more bets, Ben dropped a bunch of chips, more than he'd meant to, on number thirty-two. "Why thirty-two?" Vince growled from behind him. "I hate that number!"

"I didn't mean to put them there," Ben said, turning to look at him. "I was rushed with you whining behind me." He could have kicked himself for dropping so many chips on one number. He didn't like thirty-two either. He liked sixteen, seventeen, and twenty, always had. But then he noticed that Vince's eyes, which were not on him anymore but on the roulette wheel, were widening in astonishment. Ben turned back in time to see the little ivory-colored Delrin ball slow-ing down, then falling into the slot marked seventeen, and then, miraculously, using the last of its fire to jump out of seventeen and settle into the slot beside it: thirty-two. He turned back to Vince with his mouth dropped open and his eyes as wide as they got. "Shit," he said softly, not wanting to break the spell, "we just won a lot of money."

"How much?" Vince was licking his lips nervously.

"Three fifty, I think," Ben said, again softly, so no one standing at the table would realize that Vince was a rube. The croupier slid the winning chips toward Ben, the only winner at the table, and spun the wheel again. Ben quickly put one chip on zero, two on seventeen, and two split between seven and eight. Seventeen came in, another seventy dollars.

And so it went, for forty-five minutes or so. There were a few times none of the numbers Ben picked came up at all, but more often at least one of his bets panned out. Though Vince was nagging him from behind to place bigger bets, Ben kept to his strategy of betting no more than the mini-mum for each spin. When he lost three spins in a row, Ben assumed his luck had begun to change, at that table at least, and he tipped the croupier—modestly, it wasn't all his money—and they left the wheel.

They walked around for a while, Ben in the lead, trying to let his intuition be his guide. Finally he sat down at one of the Blackjack tables. Vince, who was afraid to make a bet there too, stood close behind him. But it wasn't happening, and after three or four losses, Ben got out of his seat and counted up their chips. That first hit on the roulette wheel had left them well ahead. They had $840, which was more than twice what they'd come downstairs with. Ben pulled his phone out of his pocket to check the time. "Listen," he said, "our luck's changed. That's what luck does. It's there and then it's not there. You can tell if you pay attention. You can feel it when it slips away. Most blue moon gamblers don't pay attention and they lose a lot of money. I'm not feeling it anymore, and I don't want to lose what we have. I'm going to count out my twenty-five percent and call it a night."

"No, way, old man," Vince cried. "Come on. Let's take a walk around other parts of the casino and see if it comes back."

Ben sighed. "We had a swell time, Vince. We doubled our money."

"It ain't gonna change things," Vince whined. "Isn't that why we came here? To try to make enough to change things for ourselves?"

"That's not how it happens. Look, I'm walking away with my share of chips. If you think you can change things by playing longer, go for it. Maybe you can. But don't come crying to me if you lose it all and you don't have enough for breakfast in the morning."

Ben counted out $110 worth of chips and handed the rest to Vince. "Fuck you," Vince said.

"Fuck you too. And remember this. If you're going to play the slots, stick to machines at the ends of rows. They tend to be looser, or so I've heard, because they're easier to see and the casino wants people to notice other people winning big. And decide ahead how much you're willing to lose before you sit down anywhere." He slapped him on the shoulder. "I'm going up for a drink in the sports bar if you need me. Good luck."

"Fuck you," Vince said again, and he walked off.

As soon as Ben entered the room, Siggy came bouncing out from under the bed nearest the door. When he reached Ben's feet, he stretched his front paws upward, just as he used to do in his younger days, and Ben picked him up and held him to his chest. "Oh, Siggy, Siggy," he sang into the cat's ear. "Oh, my sweet *sweet* boy. You're having a blast here, aren't you? Warmth and quiet and freedom. I promise you, little buddy, it won't be long until you can have this kind of luxury all the time. Daddy promises." He saw Moon's face, how she always smiled, lovingly, he thought, when he talked baby talk to any of the animals. He smiled back at her. Then his eyes filled with tears.

Derrick was sound asleep, breathing nosily though his mouth. Ben removed the remote from the foot of the bed and turned off the TV. He kissed Siggy once more and gently lowered him down beside Derrick's arm and went to the closet, where he found an extra blanket and a king-sized pillow. He unrolled his sleeping bag and set up his bedding in the corner of the room, up against the wall. He placed Siggy's carrier and his plastic trash bag along the outer edge of the sleeping bag to mark off his space. Then he dimmed the lights and quietly left the room.

He took the elevator up to the sports bar, which hadn't been built yet the last time he'd been to the casino. It was crowded and noisy up there, each of the several wall-mounted TVs on a different channel. He was turning in a circle, trying to decide whether to attempt to find a place to sit, when he espied a door on the east-facing wall. It led to a wide balcony which featured a second, much smaller bar and several lounge-style seating areas like you might find in a hotel lobby. There were only a few people scattered about. He went outside and sat down at the otherwise empty bar, and when the barmaid appeared he ordered a salad with salmon as an extra and a beer.

The air was cool and crisp up there, and the view of the Sandia Mountains was virtually unobstructed (only the resort's golf club facility lay between him and the foothills) and glorious. By the time his food arrived, the sun was beginning to set in the west, causing the Sandias, directly opposite the setting sun, to turn bright pinkish red. This happened regularly, because the Sandias were granite and the granite was full of potassium feldspar crystals, which picked up and magnified the colors of sunset. Some evenings were more intense than others. This one was nothing short of spectacular.

Ben turned sideways on his barstool to better observe the sight, which would only last for a minute or so. A few more people had gathered in the lounge areas behind him by then, and all of them had turned to look at the mountains too. The two women sitting on the catty-corner sofas closest to him had stopped chatting to stare at the sight. The thin one had her palm over her heart and looked close to tears. The chubby one was holding onto the thin one's arm, as if to steady herself in the face of such beauty. He had a flash—Moon holding onto Ruthie's arm when she told him it was time to leave. It hit him hard, but then it vanished.

The sun sank, as it had to, and the mountain quickly turned gray-brown again. Ben returned to his salad. He had pushed three of the salmon chunks to the side of his plate to save for Siggy. Now he carefully cut the crispy salt-and-peppered sides away from each of them, exposing the pure pink flesh beneath. He wrapped them in his napkin and stuck the napkin in his shirt pocket with his sunglasses.

The waitress returned from the backroom and asked him if he wanted another beer. He did, but he had promised himself he wouldn't order one. He'd gone overboard already, ordering a salad in a place like this. They had to vacate the room by eleven the next morning. If Vince blew through all his money—and Ben was almost certain he would—he'd have to pay for everyone's breakfast. It didn't make sense for the three of them to eat in the pricy casino restaurant, so they'd probably wind up grabbing something on the way back to the ledge. And since Vince's friend Sam would be driving them there, Ben would get stuck paying for Sam's breakfast too. And later Ben and Derrick and Vince would all be hungry all over again, and he'd have to pay for a second meal. And so it would go, until there was nothing left. He shrugged. There was no way around it.

One of the women from the lounge area just behind him came up to the bar and stood a few feet away from Ben, waiting for the barmaid to reappear. She held her credit card in one hand. "Beautiful evening," she said to Ben. "That's why we came here. The endless search for beauty. Neither of us gamble." She sighed. Then she laughed at herself.

Ben nodded. Already he'd lost his knack for small talk. The only small talk the homeless community engaged in regularly concerned the weather. If there was a wind coming up, or a cold front on its way in, everyone needed to know about it. But tonight he wasn't homeless. He'd had a long bath, a good meal, and he had money in his pocket. He forced himself to speak. "Yeah, it was pretty amazing."

"You visiting the area?" she asked.

The idea of him visiting anywhere made him laugh. "No, no, I live here."

"Us too. What part of town?"

He had to think about that. He *had* lived in the northwest part of the city. But the ledge was in the northeast, and that's where he lived now. "Northeast," he mumbled, "not too far from 40." In fact, he lived right under I-40. He chuckled again. That little bit of beer, the first he'd had since the night everything had gone down, had gone right to his head.

The waitress appeared, finally. "Two more?" she asked the chubby woman.

"No, just the check," she said, extending her credit card.

The waitress leaned over the bar as she took it. "Your friend doing better?" she whispered.

"Oh yeah," she said. "She's just had a streak of bad luck lately, is all."

The waitress scrunched her brows in empathy, but before the chubby woman, who was obviously prepared to provide details, could do so, she hurried into the backroom with the credit card. Naturally the chubby woman turned back to Ben. "She's my best friend," she explained.

Ben looked at her directly for the first time. She had pretty greenish-gray eyes—sparkly eyes, he thought—and her hair was a shade of auburn that looked almost natural but not quite. He figured she'd been a redhead once—she had the complexion for it—and now her hair had gone gray and she colored it to get it as close as possible to its original hue. That's what Ruthie had done. "Your best friend?" he mumbled stupidly, somehow thinking she meant the young barmaid.

The chubby woman tipped her head toward the lounge area where she'd been sitting. Ben glanced over at the skinny blonde, the one who'd placed her hand on her heart when the mountains were putting on their show. "She's a very stubborn woman," the chubby woman confided, stepping closer to him and lowering her voice.

She was waiting for him to ask, so he did. "Stubborn?"

"Stubborn as a mule." She whispered, "It's a long story, so I won't go into details, but take my word for it; she is stubborn. I love her anyway. I've known her forever." She smiled.

"Wow," Ben said, though he was totally confused. He looked back again, and this time the blonde was looking at him. She smiled and he smiled back at her, but stiffly, because he'd recognized her by then.

"Yeah, I know," the chubby woman agreed. "Lately she's been feeling sorry for herself. All her losses. She's letting it all out, a real pity party, which is a good thing now and then in my book."

"Wow," Ben said again. Where was the barmaid? Why was she taking so long? He glanced at the blonde. She looked antsy. She already had her shoulder bag strap up on her shoulder. In a minute she would walk over to see what was going on and realize that her friend was busy divulging her life story to him, a man she'd met before, a man she'd seen slinking into the homeless shelter the day her car was broadsided. She'd looked at him so hard that day. Who knew what she was thinking? Ben remembered he had his sunglasses in his pocket and quickly pulled them out, being careful not to disturb Siggy's salmon, and put them on, even though it was completely dark by then.

"Ordinarily she's the queen of stoicism, that one is," the chubby woman confided.

"Hmmm," Ben said. He looked again. The blonde was standing now, smiling in their direction but looking tense too. He thought about running, but he hadn't paid his own bill yet. Just then the barmaid returned with the check folder. The chubby woman checked the numbers, added her tip, signed her name, and removed her credit card from the plastic pocket. "Well, we're off," she said. "It was really nice to meet you." She extended her hand. "Janet," she said.

Ben shook her hand and mumbled his name. He glanced at the blonde and nodded. She nodded back. Janet whispered, "She's Lola. Though I call her Lolo sometimes, just to keep her on her toes." She winked, turned, and met up with the blonde at the glass door. As they were going through it, the blonde glanced over her shoulder and caught him staring.

Vince still wasn't back when Ben returned to the room. He wondered if he should go down to the casino and look for him. But he was tired, really tired. He wanted to crawl under his blanket on the floor and think about what it meant that he had run into that woman again, Lola. He remembered reading somewhere that Einstein once said, *Coincidence is God's way of remaining anonymous.* He was no Einstein, and he wasn't sure he believed in God, but he liked the saying and wanted his ruminations on it to carry him off into sleep.

He washed up, plugged in his phone and charger, and fed Siggy one of the salmon cubes and stored the other two in the mini refrigerator, where he discovered three bottles of water—as well as an assortment of miniature liquor bottles and some sodas. He wanted to take one of the waters, but then they'd be one short in the morning. Instead he drank a glass from the sink in the bathroom—and made a mental note not to mention the liquor bottles to Vince, who would probably want to take them home with him, not realizing that the guy whose ID they were using, Sam Brite, would get stuck paying for them. Siggy, who had been curled up beside

Derrick, let Ben settle in and then jumped off the bed and snuggled in close. *Shiraz!* Ben thought, picturing Lola standing there, the lights from indoors flickering in her over-sized glasses, her blunt cut hair, her impish smile, tall and slim in her tight jeans and dark-colored blazer.

Nobody had thought to close the curtains, and Ben awoke in time to see the sun climbing over the tops of the mountains, just as beautiful a sight as the mountain-reflected sunset the night before. It was a perfect way to end what seemed to him a perfect interlude from his homelessness. Today was the day. He would find a job, change his life. *Shiraz! Shiraz!* He'd slept well, great in fact; he rolled away from the wall with a smile on his face, hoping to hear that things had gone well for Vince too, in spite of his misgivings. But Vince wasn't there.

Ben sat up at once. Vince hadn't slept in his bed. And Derrick wasn't in his bed either. He got to his feet, went to check the bathroom. The door was wide open. No one was in there. He remembered that Vince had called his friend the day before with his phone. The number would still be on it. He could call and ask Sam Brite if he'd heard from Vince yet. But his phone was gone too, along with the charger. His jeans were folded just the way he'd left them the night before, at the foot of his bedding, but even before he reached for them, he knew he'd find the pockets empty.

9

Lola

xenia

On Sunday Lola drove to the Fernandez house with both dogs. Blue rode shotgun and Pete sat behind them in the otherwise empty van. Lola was feeling good, for the first time since the accident. Really for the first time in years, if she was honest with herself. It had been so long since she'd felt *light* that it took her some time to think of the right word to describe the sensation.

At first she didn't know what was responsible for the change she was experiencing—which felt both physical and mental. But then it came to her: she was no longer angry at George. She'd been angry with him for nine years straight, and she'd still been angry with him when he'd left her house that evening, and she'd been angry the next night when she'd gone out for drinks with Janet, and so it went for the rest of the week. But then on Saturday, her anger was gone. *Poof!* Vanished.

She couldn't think how it happened. It must have occurred during the night, almost magically, while she slept. She went to bed angry on Friday and woke up without anger on Saturday. She'd gone through the day—she'd had two groomings in the morning and a training session with the employees of the local Pets Galore in the afternoon—marveling at how unlike herself she felt without her anger, as if she'd forgotten to put on a coat that she wore daily and was only just realizing she'd never needed. Now it seemed inconceivable to her that she'd lived with anger for so long. It occurred to her that anger was, in her case at least, the counterpart to vulnerability. We all feel vulnerable on some level all the time, but when someone we love does something that devastates us, we express our utter helplessness with anger. In essence, anger was love turned inside out. Without her anger, she felt nothing but love, for George especially.

This new-found clarity seemed to shift her awareness to everything around her, every*one* around her—significantly. The world she walked through now seemed good to her—in spite of her absolute belief that we were all endangered species living on a planet that would not tolerate us much longer.

Forgetting what George had done was not really possible, she realized, but forgiving what she would never forget was. Forgiving in the face of being unable to forget was an act of compassion which she now knew she was capable of performing. She'd sent a text message to George, who was back in Miami, just before she left the house with Pete and Blue. It read, *I forgive you, I forgive you absolutely. I just wanted you to know.* She didn't feel it necessary to say anything more. They were on different paths. His, unfortunately, would carry him to his death. She was sure he had plenty of friends in Miami, as well as therapists, caregivers, a full support system. He was one of those people everyone liked. He didn't need her interaction. She would love him from afar, as, she realized now, she always had. She just needed to let him know this *thing* had occurred, and he could go on in whatever time he had left knowing that she no longer held a grudge against him. She didn't even feel it necessary to tell him that she had also forgiven herself. That was really beside the point. He must have understood all this for himself, because he texted back only two words: *Thank you.*

She thought about all this as she drove into the South Valley with the pups, and she thought about the other curious thing that had happened that week, when she'd agreed to go with Janet to a bar located in the local casino resort and she'd seen that man again, the one she'd seen that hot summer day of her accident, slinking into the homeless shelter dressed in a winter jacket. Obviously he wasn't homeless. And he probably wasn't a terrorist either. Anyway, he hadn't blown up the shelter or she'd have heard about it. Maybe he worked there. Or maybe he was a volunteer. She could imagine a man like him volunteering to help homeless people. He looked, well, kind, thoughtful. Or, maybe the man at the bar was the doppelgänger of the one she'd seen at the shelter. That was possible too. Ben, Janet said his name was. Ben was handsome, Lola thought. His whitish beard was perfectly trimmed. His dark brown hair was combed back into a short ponytail. If Janet had not insisted on paying the bar bill, it would have been her standing there beside Ben waiting for the barmaid to reappear. She wondered if she would have had the nerve to ask him if he knew he had a doppelgänger. Probably not. It sounded rather like a lame pickup line. It probably would have embarrassed him. Janet said he seemed shy.

She'd never asked Jamie Hernandez's daughter what her name was. She could kick herself for that now. Her plan was to leave the dogs in the van and go in, if invited to do so, and visit with the girl and her grandmother for a short time and then bring the girl out to meet Pete and Blue. She'd bought a gift for the girl, a silver charm for her bracelet. It had taken her forever to choose the right one. There were suns and moons and hearts and animals and religious- and hobby-related charms aplenty at the jewelry store, but each seemed to insinuate something about what Lola hoped for their relationship, and she didn't want to appear to imply any purpose at all. She didn't have one, really. In the end she bought a leaf, a beautiful sterling silver leaf, its midrib and veins articulated. It didn't seem to say anything beyond, *Here I am, beautiful but without motive or expectations.* If the girl wanted to apply a meaning to it, she could do that on her own.

The girl was sitting outside on the concrete stoop when Lola turned into the driveway. She hadn't expected that. Nor had she expected Blue, whose behavior was improving by the day, to leap over her as soon as she opened the door and rush out. She thought for sure the girl would think Blue was attacking, but then she saw the girl's mouth open with delight just before Blue knocked her back and began to cover her face with kisses. "I'm so sorry," Lola cried, running to grab his collar. "I wasn't even going to let them out of the van."

"Them?" the girl asked, sitting up, one eyebrow cocked. She was wearing a red t-shirt with a big blue happy face in the center. "How many you got in there?"

"Just one more."

"Can I see?"

Lola walked back to the van and opened the sliding door and Pete jumped down. Ever the gentleman, he walked slowly to the stranger and sat in front of her, as if for inspection. "This is Pete," Lola said. "The naughty one is Blue."

The girl put her hand out and Pete gave her his paw. She shook it. "I'm Karen," she told him. So, Karen. Karen Hernandez. She was pretty when she smiled.

"We should go in," Karen said. "She's waiting and you're late."

Late? Lola didn't recall them ever setting a time. After church, Karen had said. How was she supposed to know what time they went to church? She shepherded the dogs back to the van, checked that the windows were cracked, and closed the door behind them. When she turned, Karen was holding the screen door wide open, waiting for her.

"My grandmother's name is Rosa," Karen said as they walked into the small living room. "Remember that she doesn't speak English. I'll translate if she says anything. Sometimes she won't. It depends on her mood."

Lola nodded and followed behind, taking in an arrangement of artificial flowers in a brown ceramic bowl on a coffee table, a dark red sweetheart-style sofa fitted with a plastic cover, and end tables covered with photos in plexiglass frames, mostly black and white and in a variety of sizes. Surely some of them were of Jamie, but she didn't want to look too hard. She was here to get to know him, through his mother and his daughter. She didn't want to see his teardrop tattoo or any other markings that would quell her good intentions. She stepped into the small dining room, in the middle of which was a rectangular table covered with an embroidered cloth and flanked by four straight-back chairs. To her surprise, plates (scalloped edges, a sequence of rose designs dotting the lips) had been set out along with pink cloth napkins and utensils.

Rosa emerged from the kitchen just then, moving slowly, a basket of bread in one hand while she used the other to grab onto a series of handrails—the kind you see in bathrooms—that someone had installed for her along all the walls of the dining room and the part of the kitchen Lola could see from where she stood. "Good morning," Lola said. Rosa put the basket down on the table and pointed to the chair at the end of the table and Lola sat.

Rosa went slowly back into the kitchen and returned with a plate of bacon, then back again for a bowl of packaged jams and syrups that must have come from IHOP. Lola wanted to help the old lady, but Karen had sat down beside her and was peppering her with questions. Did she live nearby? Did she have her own house? Did she have more pets at home? And all the while Rosa floated back and forth in the background, like an apparition, and more and more food appeared on the table—scrambled eggs, baked tomatoes, chili peppers, posole. Lola, who had not expected to be served a meal, let alone a feast, had already eaten a bowl of oatmeal at home. Impossibly, and fortunately, she found herself hungry again.

"My job?" she asked. She'd only been half listening to Karen, who was proving herself to be quite the interrogator. "I groom dogs. Sometimes I foster them and train them and give them to families who are looking for dogs they won't have to train themselves."

Rosa jerked her chair until it was as close to Lola's as possible and sat, finally, and began passing the plates around. Karen translated what Lola had just said—or so Lola assumed. Then Rosa asked a question and Karen translated into English. "Grandma wants to know if you're married and how many kids you have."

Now that was a hard one. She'd already mentioned she had a daughter who'd died when she'd been there the week before, but she'd said it to Rosa, who probably hadn't understood, and she didn't feel like going there again. To buy time, Lola focused on taking a little food from each of the plates being passed to her. When the bread basket came her way—the bread was warm, hearty, obviously homemade—she took a big slice and bit into it. She made humming noises, to let Rosa know how much she liked it, then moved her head side to side to indicate that she couldn't answer because she was too busy chewing. Finally she swallowed and said the only thing she could think of that would bypass any need to mention Valerie. "My husband is retired, but he used to be a Foley artist. Do you know what that is?" She didn't see the point in mentioning that she and George were divorced and that he was dying in another state.

Karen translated. Rosa shrugged. Karen shrugged back at her. "What's a Foley artist?" she asked.

Lola explained, slowly—so that Karen could translate and Rosa, who seemed interested, could follow along—that Foley was an art form used to create various sounds for movies and television shows. "Say you're watching a TV show," she said, "and you see two people talking at a table when a knock comes at the door. The viewer needs to hear that, even though they can't see it."

Karen translated. The old lady regarded Lola skeptically while she chewed—small tight movements that seemed to involve only her front teeth. Then she spoke. Karen said, "She wants to know why you need an artist to knock on the door. What's so artistic about that?"

Lola laughed. "Maybe you want a richer, more threatening sound than the one someone offstage made initially.

There are all kinds of sound effects that might be needed to match—to enhance, really—the movement on the screen after the fact. The right sounds can bring added drama to a story. Actors don't really hit each other hard when they reenact a fight, for instance. The Foley artist makes the real fight sounds for them by slapping his own arms and hands, sometimes while wearing heavy gloves. I'm saying he, but women can be Foley artists too. Of course."

She and George had moved out to New Mexico so he could get into the state's flourishing film industry. He'd never wanted to act. He wanted to work behind the scenes. He'd done some camera work for a while, but he was happiest when he switched to Foley.

"Or he might put on a coat and slap himself," Lola continued, "depending on what the actors are wearing. Or say some men are having a sword fight. You know how a sword makes swooshing noises when the person wielding it is about to strike? The Foley artist can make that same sound by waving a wooden dowel in the air, much safer for the actors involved, as you can imagine. Or what if the actor needs to break someone's bones? You can break a couple of crisp celery stalks to make that sound. It's much more complicated than I'm explaining. The sounds get layered together during the edits."

Rosa listened to the translation and then jerked her head toward the kitchen and Karen jumped up and ran in and returned seconds later with a stalk of celery and handed it to the old lady. "She wants you to pretend to break my arm," Karen said.

"Oh my," Lola exclaimed. It seemed a bit of an inappropriate request. But then there was Karen's arm in front of her and there was Rosa getting ready to snap the celery stalk. Lola took a deep breath and nodded when she was ready and

Rosa snapped the stalk and at the same time Lola made a fierce face and pretended to break Karen's arm and Karen swooned to the floor crying in pain, and when she popped up again everyone had a good long laugh.

And so went the next hour. Karen said she would want to be a Foley artist herself if she hadn't already decided to be a designer. Lola asked what she wanted to design, and Karen left the room and returned with a thick watercolor notebook full of drawings of girls and women of various shapes, sizes, and skin colors wearing clothes that Karen had created for them. They were lovely. They were the kind of unpretentious comfort clothes that Lola wore all the time. She oohed and aahed over each of them while Karen leaned over her shoulder. Midway through the notebook it occurred to her that Rosa might be feeling left out, but when she glanced at her, she saw the old woman was smiling with pride. "Do you study this in high school?" Lola asked.

"Nah, we have art, but not designing clothes art."

"Will you study it in college?"

"Yeah. Some teachers are helping me. I might get a scholarship."

"Oh, that's wonderful. These are beautiful. You're going to be very successful."

Karen smiled broadly and ran out of the room to put the book away. When she returned, Rosa got up to clear the table. Lola got up too and gathered some plates and tried to get into the kitchen with them, but Karen blocked her way while Rosa, who was scraping some food scraps from a plate into a compost bucket, scolded her in Spanish. "She said you're a guest and guests don't get to help clean up in this house. Just sit. It will only be a few minutes. We won't wash until later, after you're gone."

Lola sat back down and watched the plates disappear from the table. Once the table was clear, Karen took her seat again, and when Lola mumbled something about how she should be going soon, Karen silenced her with a finger. "Grandma went to get something," she whispered.

Rosa reentered the room carrying a carved wooden box, maybe seven inches long and three or four inches high. She had to walk especially slowly because she needed both hands to support it and couldn't use the grab rails. She sat down and eased the box in Lola's direction and signaled that Lola should open it.

Lola ran her fingertips over the carvings on the top. She'd seen the design before. In fact, it was quite common: a tree of life in a circle, surrounded by flowers and other fili-gree. Lola remembered having such a box herself years ago. She believed they were made in India, from rosewood. Rosa had handled the box reverently, as if it were of great value. So as not to appear ungracious, Lola did the same, lifting the lid inchmeal, again using only her fingertips.

Inside it were polished stones, seashells, some coins, some keys, a ring or two—keepsakes. Lola looked up to see that Rosa and Karen were watching her closely. She wasn't sure what she was expected to do. She was drawn to a green calcite palm stone. She lifted it out and rubbed her fingertips over its smooth surface. She was about to replace it when Rosa's hand appeared. She closed the lid and pulled the box back toward her. Lola extended the stone, but Rosa shook her head. "She wants you to have it," Karen whispered rever-ently.

"Thank you," Lola said, somewhat mystified, looking from Karen to Rosa. "Thank you for this and for a wonderful breakfast." She lifted out of her seat. She wanted to hug the old lady but she was lifting too, then gliding toward the kitchen with the aid of the handrails. She nodded in Lola's direction but didn't stop moving.

Karen didn't seem to want a hug either. She walked Lola out to the van, stuck her head in long enough to nuzzle each of the dogs, both of whom were squeezed together on the driver's seat, and then skipped back to the house, as if she didn't have a care in the world, as if she were nine or ten rather than a teenager.

Lola was already down the street when she realized she hadn't given Karen her gift, the charm for her bracelet. She made a U-turn and went back, but not wanting to bother Karen or her grandmother, she drove up to the mounted mailbox there on the road and slipped the small box inside. She hadn't asked a single question about Jamie either, another intention down the drain. The old woman had lost a son and Karen had lost a father, and Lola had gone there hoping to express her condolences and learn more about the man. Nothing of the sort had happened. The issue remained unresolved.

As she drove along the quiet back streets that she preferred to the highways, Lola realized that not only had she neglected to ask about Jamie, but she hadn't even introduced herself. No one had asked her name. She'd gone in a stranger and she'd left a stranger—a stranger with a gift, the pretty green stone. It seemed surrealistic to her that the day had not gone at all as she had imagined it would. *Be water*, she thought. It was a quote from Bruce Lee, the martial arts legend. She used to say it to Valerie when she was overthinking a situation.

10

BEN
melancholia

Ben didn't have to vacate the room for another hour. He'd already showered, split what was left of the salmon chucks with Siggy, drank down one of the three bottles of water from the refrigerator and packed the other two into his backpack. Now he sat on the edge of the bed that Vince had never bothered to sleep in, deliberating over whether or not he should steal its down comforter. It would add bulk to his bag, especially if he kept it in its duvet cover, but it might be the carrot that would get Vince to give him back his phone. The phone was everything. He'd never find a job without it.

He walked west, to the north-south bike trail that ran parallel to the highway. He had ten or so miles to do on the trail and then another half mile through the field to get to the east-west trail that led to the ledge. If not for the fact that he was weighed down with his sleeping bag, backpack, cat carrier, heavier-than-ever trash bag, and a surplus of woe, he could have jogged the distance in a couple of hours. As it was, he had to stop every quarter mile or so just to rearrange his load.

Though he was clean and in clean clothes, the people out on their bikes on the trail eyed him suspiciously and kept their distance when they had to pass him. He tried not to notice. He was concentrating. He had to perfect his argument. He was angry, very angry, but it wouldn't do to show it. He had the down comforter; Vince would want it. At the very least maybe they could agree to share the phone. If Vince wasn't calling every thug he knew or surfing the internet, the charge might last another day—enough time for him to find a job, any job.

But what if Vince refused? For the first time since he'd become homeless he considered the possibility that he would never get a job, that he would remain homeless for the rest of his life. And surely he would die sooner than later, from disease or by accident—an abscessed tooth was enough to end things for a man who couldn't afford a dentist—out on the filthy ledge surrounded by dirty pigeons and the sickening *rumble/clang/thump thump* of trucks passing overhead.

He tried to think back to the succession of events that had brought him to this moment—not so much the scene at Gino's and his time in jail—those he'd already run through his head more times than was healthy for a man who hoped to hang on to what was left of his sanity—but afterwards, the events that led directly to his homelessness. Ruthie had pledged her support in the beginning, and so had Moon. That was beautiful; that was what he'd needed. He was innocent, they knew that. He'd made a grave mistake—*grave*, Ruthie's word, and she used it every time; in her mouth it was always italicized when she uttered it, an octave lower than the sentences it was wrapped in—but they swore they would not let it ruin their family, the "us" that required the allegiance of all three of them in order to exist. Ruthie was the one who found him the lawyer, in fact—Justin Prescott, a man who was a regular at the acupuncture center where she worked. Prescott praised him for having such a supportive wife. He said it would take time. And of course money. But it would work out.

But then things changed. Ruthie's friends, and even some of the clients she knew from the center, offered her only sympathy in the beginning. Soon after, though, they began to offer advice. They told her horror stories, over the phone or when they stopped at her desk to pay their bill after their session. They knew someone, or they knew someone who knew someone, a woman who had lost everything, *everything*, because of her spouse's grave mistakes. Ruthie should get her own lawyer, they said. She should have a document drawn up declaring that she was severing her legal ties with Ben. Better yet, she should divorce him. They could always marry again later. In the meantime, a divorce would help to ensure that her share of their assets was protected.

Ben agreed. He told Prescott, thinking to have him handle the sham divorce for Ruthie's sake. But Prescott didn't like the idea at all. He said they should wait to file any divorce papers, because it would hurt his case if he and Ruthie were unable to present a united front from the get-go.

Ruthie was torn. She wanted to present a united front, of course she did. But who knew how things would go? It could take a couple of years, everyone said, before there was a final verdict. In the meantime, and in accordance with the laws of New Mexico, which was considered a "community property state," all debt belonged to Ruthie and Ben equally.

Ruthie got her own lawyer, a fierce woman by the name of Sharon Peel, and the divorce proceedings began. The documents Peel drew up—and Ben signed—awarded the house and most of their savings to Ruthie. To justify Ruthie getting the greater part of their savings, meager though it was, Peel had Ben sign an affidavit stating that most of what they had had come from Ruthie by inheritance. Was it true? Ben didn't know. She had inherited a little something when her father died. It was a long time ago; he didn't remember how much or when. It didn't matter. He wanted Ruthie and Moon to be protected as much as possible. Why should they stand to lose anything? After all, it was his grave mistake.

But Peel didn't stop there. She had seen the footage of Ben wearing his bloody shirt on his head, of him being pushed into the back of the squad car, his face not remorseful but outraged, his lips curled in an ugly way, his bared teeth, his hateful glare—and she had no doubt the jurors would be made to see it too. She personally thought Ruthie would be better protected from any kind of incrimination if Ben found himself another place to live, at least until after the trial. Ruthie listened to her arguments, but in the end she couldn't bring herself to go that far. Ben would be hard put to pay his legal fees as it was, let alone to pay to live elsewhere. But she did ask him move into the third bedroom—for the sake of appearances.

They argued about that. *Why?* he asked. *Do you really expect agents to come to the house and check to see where I sleep? Just do it*, she said. *Just do it because I asked you to, because it makes me more comfortable.* And so he moved into what had formerly been the junk room. He pushed the table that held the sewing machine she never used into a corner and stored all the boxes of fabric and buttons and bows beneath it. There were three old computers in there; he piled them up on boxes that contained empty picture frames and moved the treadmill, which he'd meant to fix, up against them. Then he filled six boxes with the books that were scattered in piles around the room and turned them into six posts. He found an old twin-size mattress out in the shed. He washed it down and let it dry out in the sun and placed it on the book-box posts. He got an old lamp to work again so he could at least read in there.

That—not the sham divorce—was the true beginning of the end of their marriage.

He reached the overpass he called home some four hours later. He left his trash bag, backpack, and sleeping bag up at the top and climbed down to the ledge with Siggy's carrier. You couldn't actually see the ledge from up top: you had to slide down the embankment a few feet and land on the ledge. And because there was no head space, you had to bend right away and go in head first, with whatever you were carrying out in front of you. Ben dropped down and bent and immediately found himself face to face with the end of a strand of razor wire. He couldn't believe his eyes. It reached all the way across the ledge, right to the far end. It had to have been installed during the short time he'd been gone, yesterday afternoon or earlier that day. Miraculously, he hadn't walked right into it. If he had, his face would have been cut to shreds. But the carrier had gotten snagged. Ben jumped back, horrified that it might have cut through the fabric and injured Siggy.

Had Vince known the razor wire installation was coming? No, how could he have?

The thing was a monster slinky full of barbs. Already some plastic bags had attached themselves to it. So had a pigeon. He was hanging from the razor wire by one wing. He wasn't moving. He was probably dead.

Ben couldn't stop staring at him. Pigeons' spatial perception was off the charts. How had this guy let himself get caught like that? Right behind the spot where he dangled was Owl, sitting where he always sat, patiently waiting for Derrick to return, now forever imprisoned there.

Ben crawled back up to where he'd left his stuff and got Siggy out of the carrier. He turned him every which way while rubbing his fingers through his fur, tears of gratitude forming in his eyes when he saw there wasn't a scratch on him. Then he noticed that one leg of his jeans had ripped and his damn leg was bleeding.

He put Siggy on the ground and gave him some water, keeping one foot over the end of the leash while he examined the carrier. The tear was maybe four inches long; if he could get some duct tape on it, it should hold, for a while at least. He attached the leash to the carrier and put the carrier down on the ground, so that Siggy could move around more freely. Hopefully he would relieve himself quickly. If Ben wanted any chance of a meal at the shelter, he was going to have to head that way soon. He only hoped Nancy would be there to watch Siggy while he ran in.

But now he had this other problem. His leg was bleeding pretty good. He pulled his jeans down to his ankles, right there along I-40, and found a t-shirt in his trash bag and tied it around his leg. Then he pulled his jeans back up, placed Siggy, who had just finished doing his business, back in his carrier, picked up the rest of his stuff, and started walking.

He had never felt suicidal before, not even when Ruthie threw him out, not even when Moon told him to fuck himself. Somehow he had always thought he could resolve those problems, that once he found a job and got back on his feet again, Moon would forgive him and Ruthie would come to tolerate him. Just as he'd examined Siggy inch by inch for any cuts from the razor wire, he examined himself now for any suicidal inclinations. All men had a breaking point. He imagined his as a roadblock, an orange and white wooden structure that could be seen from a distance, giving the person approaching some time to search for other options. He could see his roadblock ahead, in his mind. Like the dumb pigeon, he had lost his spatial perspective. He couldn't tell how far off it was.

He wondered what it had been like for Derrick to see his owl trapped behind the razor wire. Here the owl was supposed to be scaring off the pigeons, and instead he had attracted one. Or maybe the pigeon had been thinking to attack Owl, seeing that his buddy had abandoned him. And now he would have to live out his life—he was plastic; he would live forever—with his natural enemy (or whatever would eventually remain of him) dangling not a foot away from him.

Ben considered that his brain might not be fully functional anymore. Probably Vince and Derrick had never even gone back to the ledge. Why would they have? Vince had robbed him. He must have weighed the situation and decided that Ben's money and phone were worth more than a good night's sleep in a clean bed. He'd seen Ben's dark side that day out on the field. He'd be on the run for a while now. Who knew what would become of poor Derrick?

As he neared the shelter, he saw Nancy talking to some of the other women outside the building and at once he began to cry. He couldn't help himself. He hadn't known it was about to happen. She saw him approaching and broke off from the group. "What's going on?" she exclaimed. "Why do you have all your stuff with you?"

"They still serving?" he asked. "Can we talk after I eat?"

"Yeah, yeah, but hurry up in, Ben. They're almost done." She took the carrier from him and set it down against the brick wall and then sat down on the sidewalk right beside it. He placed the trash bag and his sleeping bag and backpack next to her. "Go, go," she urged.

Ten minutes later he was back out. Nancy had already removed Siggy's bowl from the carrier's pocket, and Ben poured in some of the milk from the half-pint carton he'd gotten with his meal. Dinner had been spicy beef tacos, not on Siggy's diet. But Ben had used a Styrofoam bowl to swipe a good amount of grated Monterey from the toppings counter.

"So what happened?" Nancy asked as Ben unzipped the carrier door and leashed up his cat.

He studied her face. With the setting sun low in the sky and her features scrunched up in concern, there were more lines than he usually noticed. Didn't matter. It was still a beautiful open face. "I hit bottom," he said matter-of-factly. "Vince took off with my phone. Someone covered the ledge with razor wire. I ripped my only pair of decent jeans, and I cut my damn leg. I'm done, Nance. I'm out of ideas."

"I heard about the ledge. One of the girls told me that some woman riding her bike on the trail complained to the city about someone up on the ledge throwing rocks at her."

Ben shook his head. "Vince. It was a while ago. At least the one time I saw him. Maybe he threw others I never knew about."

"Bastard," Nancy mumbled.

Ben looked into her blue eyes. "Nance, I have nowhere to sleep tonight."

She stared back at him for a long time, and then something in her eyes shifted. "I can't help, Ben," she said. Her tone had shifted too, and her voice had gone down an octave. "Mrs. Quick, the woman who lets me park my car in her driveway, would never stand for it. That's all I have. You have to understand that."

"I do, I do. I'm not asking for myself. But Siggy … You could take Siggy, right? Until I figure things out?"

She looked down at the cat, who was just finishing his milk. He'd only eaten a little of the cheese. She reached into her bag and pulled out a small plastic bag, a Ziploc. Nancy always seemed to have whatever the moment called for right there, on her person. She was like a girl scout in that way. She dumped the remaining cheese into the bag hastily and zipped it shut and handed it to Ben.

"Just for a couple of nights. I'll have a plan by then. I have to."

Nancy sighed and got up from the sidewalk and dusted off her backside. "Come on," she said, lifting his sleeping bag.

Her car was across the street, a beige 2005 Jetta with plenty of scars and an ugly dent on the back left side. She put the sleeping bag down at her feet and opened the trunk. It was nearly full: spare tire, three gray canvas suitcases that had seen better days, a hairdryer with the cord wrapped around the handhold, several reusable grocery bags—all of them stuffed to the top with smaller possessions. She fumbled around in one of the bags and produced a small plastic first aid kit. "Fully stocked," she said handing it to him. "Gauze, scissors, disinfectant, the works. You can give it back to me tomorrow." She sighed again, loudly. "Okay, whatever you don't need to carry, try to fit it in here. It'll make it easier for you to get around. I can't put anything in the back seat, though. That's my stuff that I need to have close at hand daily."

He looked at her. Her tone had definitely changed. He was an annoyance now. For a moment he was lost, adrift, and a moment later he was in the kitchen with Ruthie. He'd made her something special; maybe it was the night he made the lemon chicken, from a recipe he'd found on the internet. *You like it?* he'd asked. *Hmmm*, she said, *good.* But her tone said the opposite. Her tone said she preferred silence. Her eyes never strayed from her plate. He remembered looking at Moon. She was pushing food around on her plate. She didn't want to be there with them anymore.

He forced himself to concentrate. His trash bag would fit in the trunk in a spot between two of Nancy's suitcases if he took out the comforter. He didn't want her to know he was a thief, but he didn't want to haul around more than he had to. He removed it. He stuffed the trash bag into the spot he'd identified and then fit the comforter over top of everything. Nancy watched but didn't say a word. When he was done, she slammed the trunk closed. "What do I need to do with Siggy?" she asked.

If he wasn't imagining it, her tone was actually bitter now. If it continued to devolve, she'd be screaming at him next. Apparently, Nancy needed him to acknowledge the degree to which he was putting her out. He understood. In the world of the down-and-outers, you didn't ask for favors. Everyone had what little they did because they'd fought for it. Or stolen it. Dog eat dog. Or as Moon used to say when she was little, Dog-y-dog. "Nothing," he said. "Just let him out once before you go to bed. On his leash. Give him a few minutes to pee. He did the other before. He'll be okay through the night."

"Okay, say goodbye then. I'll meet you here in the morning, at eight. Please be on time. I have my shrink tomorrow. I can't be late. I only get a half hour with her as it is."

He opened the passenger door and placed the carrier on the seat. Then he bent over it, his face up against its mesh door, and whispered something to his cat. When he straightened, he had tears in his eyes again. He didn't bother to wipe them away. He didn't care what Nancy thought. He didn't care what anyone thought. He didn't care about anything except Siggy and, now that he'd let her back into his head, Moon.

"I don't know how to thank you," he said tonelessly.

"We'll think of something," she said, her blue eyes as hard as marbles.

The comforter. He nodded. He'd probably never see Vince again anyway.

11

LOLA

salvation

Lola had a wooden baker's rack in the corner of her kitchen. It featured three wide shelves from the middle point to the bottom and a smaller shelf at top from which hung several S hooks. Long ago she'd nailed side boards alongside the lower shelves, so that she could keep her cookbooks on them without having to rely on bookends. She used the small shelf at top to hold oil and vinegar bottles and salt and pepper shakers, and she hung potholders from the S hooks. These were potholders she never used, because Valerie had made them. Lola and George had bought her a loom and bags of colored cotton loops when she was nine or ten, and for the next couple of years she made potholders for everyone, for every occasion.

Presently all the cookbooks and potholders and bottles and shakers were on the table, because Lola was painting the baker's rack bright orange. Orange had been Valerie's favorite color, and she had used it liberally in her potholder designs. It was those neon orange loops that had inspired Lola to choose the color for the rack.

Lola counted among her friends two women who had daughters around the same age (twenty-seven) Valerie would have been now if she hadn't died: Carol, the friend who had published Lola's poetry chapbook; and Sophie, a woman who had been bringing her two border collies to Lola for grooming for years. Carol's daughter Emma lived in Utah. She'd been married twice, but neither relationship had panned out. She had a good job working as an event coordinator for some big hotel in Salt Lake City, but she was tired of it and always on the lookout for something more exciting.

Carol and Emma spoke almost daily. Whenever Lola asked how Emma was doing, Carol always had a fresh and specific answer. *Tuesday she went on a first date with someone she met on a dating site, but the guy had a bad habit of continuously clearing his throat and Emma couldn't deal with it*, Carol had said when she and Lola had had lunch together a few months ago, and over the phone, more recently, *She's upset because she gained four pounds; she's seeing a nutritionist to try to figure out what's going on.*

Sophie's daughter was just the opposite. Leslie lived right in town, but Sophie only saw her occasionally and they hardly ever spoke on the phone. Whenever Lola asked how Leslie was doing, Sophie answered non-specifically. Leslie was still teaching anthropology at the university; she and Jeff, her husband of some five years now, were doing fine, *paying down their post-grad loans, saving for a down payment for a house. So and so's birthday was coming up soon, and she guessed they'd all get together then.*

If Valerie had lived, Lola wondered as she painted, would she have wanted a strong and continuous bond with Lola, a best-of-friends relationship like Carol had with Emma? Or would she have been aloof, like Leslie? Lola knew from a few comments Sophie had made over the years that Sophie wished her daughter confided in her more. Once she admitted she sometimes wondered if Leslie and her husband even *liked* her, as a person. They hugged her when they got together; they said *love you too* when Sophie said it first, but their words sounded flat to her, obligatory. "What can you do?" Sophie had said one day in Lola's shop. "You can't tell your grown kids to love you more. That would only backfire and make them love you less. You have to take what you get."

Lola supposed it was because Leslie had Jeff in her life, and a career she loved and a wide circle of friends. If Emma's circumstances had been different, if she had a partner and a job she enjoyed, maybe she'd be less forthcoming too. Or maybe not; maybe Leslie was simply remote and Emma wasn't. Or maybe Leslie really *didn't* love her mom.

Valerie was just short of her seventeenth birthday when she died; the kind of mother-daughter relationship they would have had if she had lived was virtually impossible to gauge. And Val wasn't herself in the months leading up to her death anyway. She'd stopped talking to Lola and George about her day-to-day challenges and achievements by then. But she did seem to be developing a social life, something she hadn't had for a few years. Lola and George could only assume she was sharing her life experiences with her friends, which was to be expected.

They were happy at first when Valerie said she was invited to stay at the home of this or that girl on a Friday night. In fact, they had to curb their reaction; they didn't want her to suspect they'd been worried sick that she'd been wandering around in an isolating depression. They told themselves—and each other—that she was at that age when kids got moody at home, with their families, when they begin to feel the need for some separation. It was normal. It would be okay. She had friends now. She'd be fine.

When she appeared in the kitchen after dinner on a Friday evening with her overnight bag, they'd ask whose home she was going to and always she mentioned names that were somewhat familiar to them. When they asked if they could drive her to her destination, she always said no, that her friend was picking her up, or, if her friend didn't drive yet either (Valerie still had only a provisional license), that her friend's older sister was coming to get her. Then she'd walk to the park, always the park, the same park from which a hawk had once chased her. Everyone hung out there, she said. The advantage of being picked up in the park was that you could talk to other kids, find out what they were doing, while you were waiting for your ride. When she came home the next day, usually mid-morning, they would inquire, as casually as possible, what she and Joy or she and Stephie or she and Samantha had done. They'd played badminton in Joy's backyard until it got dark and then told ghost stories until they fell asleep, or they'd helped Stephie's mother to wrap holiday gifts and then went to another girl's house on the same street to dance to some CDs she had, or she and Samantha had taken turns drawing each other. *Why don't the girls ever come here?* George asked once, after Val had left the room. Lola shrugged. She didn't know the answer.

One Saturday morning Lola and George awoke to the horrible sound of a tree falling somewhere behind their house, the groan and crack and reverberant boom. Lola's hand shot out and clamped down on George's wrist like a vice. "I'll go see," he whispered hoarsely.

Hoping it hadn't fallen on their shed, George put on a t-shirt and sweatpants—out of habit he slipped his cell phone into his back pocket—and hurried outside. The tree— a forty-plus-foot honey locust—hadn't fallen on anything, not even another tree, but he stood there for a while, marveling at the size and complexity of its root system, which was almost as big as the canopy itself. There had been no wind, so what could have caused it to fall over? He noticed that the bark around the base looked wet: collar rot, he guessed. He walked in the treed area at the back of the property frequently; how could he have failed to notice that this tree was sick? Lola especially loved the tree, whose leaves were bright yellow-green in summer. Sometimes she took a book and sat beneath it. If he had noticed before, he could have tried cleaning away the organic matter from the base of the trunk. Maybe the tree would have lived a few more years. Or he could have called in a specialist to see if there were other solutions.

He turned and headed back to his house. He glanced at the bedroom window and saw Lola standing there, her distress at the loss of her favorite tree apparent in the way she held her hand on her mouth. He glanced at the shed window as he passed and saw what looked like one bare foot in the sliver of space between the curtain panels. One bare foot. That stopped him in his tracks.

Valerie, alone, on a blanket, fully dressed except for her feet, her pink running shoes side by side next to her overnight bag. How had she not heard the tree go down?

He knocked, but she didn't get up. The door was locked from the inside; he had to kick it in, and she didn't hear that either. Before he even got to her he was phoning Lola, telling her to call an ambulance, call the police.

One Ziploc containing eight greenish-blue pills. Fentanyl, the police said. Probably counterfeit, but they'd have to check to be sure. No evidence of foul play. No evidence that anyone else had been with her at all.

No one at school knew she had a problem. No one knew where she might have gotten the drugs. No one admitted to having spent time with her in, *oh, gee, maybe three years.* No one had ever seen her in the park waiting for a ride on a Friday evening. No answers anywhere. Only a pileup of questions, the main one of which was, *How could we have failed her so?*

The phone rang. Lola balanced her brush on her paint can to answer it. "Can I come over?" Janet asked.

Lola had to laugh. Janet was the friend version of the day-to-day daughter. "I'll open the front door," she said.

As she got up off her knees and went into the living room she realized that she had been thinking about Valerie for the last hour or so without the stab of grief that usually accompanied her thoughts. She'd experienced curiosity while wondering what kind of young woman Val would have been, and sadness remembering the circumstances of her death. But her thoughts had come and gone and there did not seem to be any feeling of utter devastation lurking anywhere. *Humph.*

She opened the door. Both dogs knew that when Lola got a call and went to the door immediately thereafter, it could only mean one thing: Janet was coming. They got down from the sofa and stood side by side in front of the screen door, so as to be able to watch Janet magically appear outside her gate. Their tails wagged in anticipation of the moment. Although Janet never did more than pat them on the head, they seemed to like her immensely.

Back in the kitchen, Lola looked at the baker's rack. She sighed. She'd painted the sides the night before, two coats, and they were dry. Today she'd done a second coat on the three lower shelves. It was as good a time as any to take a break.

When Janet walked in, Lola was rinsing her brush in the sink. She turned, expecting to see Janet with her mouth agape, horrified and somehow personally offended by the orange paint. But Janet wasn't even looking at the baker's rack or the stuff piled all over the table. She was looking at Lola, beseechingly. Her bottom lip was quivering; she was clearly on the verge of tears. "What?" Lola cried.

"Coffee first, please," Janet croaked, dropping down onto her chair.

Lola poured from the pot and nuked her a cup. "What is it, Janet? Tell me."

"Something's wrong in my head," Janet wailed.

Lola pushed the cookbooks aside and moved her chair next to Janet's.

"Yesterday," Janet said. She must have remembered then that Lola had gone to the Hernandez house yesterday because she looked up, blinking back tears, and squeaked out a question. "Did you take both dogs with you after all?"

Lola nodded. Janet had made a fuss about the possibility of her taking both dogs. She'd tried to get Lola to change her mind. "Yes, but tell me about you first. You went to Lynnie's yesterday, right? Did something happen there?"

Lynnie and her husband Fred lived high up in the foothills, in a beautiful pueblo revival-style house that Janet greatly admired. Its huge indoor-outdoor space all along the back side was home to a second kitchen, a sizable bar, a heated pool, a hot tub, a pool table, a stone fireplace and various dining and seating areas, all protected from the weather by a roof and three walls of retractable glass patio doors and overlooking—depending on where you stood—the valley below or the mountains to the northeast. Lynnie and Fred had parties all the time, and Janet was always invited—and Lola too, by extension. Lola had gone a few times. "My mind shut down, yesterday while I was there," Janet mumbled.

"Were you smoking pot again?" Lynnie had been getting high regularly since her high school days. She was used to it. She could function just as well high as she could not. That had never been the case for Janet, or Lola, or Fred for that matter.

"Yes, and drinking champagne too, but still …"

Lola laughed. "That's what minds do when confronted with pot and champagne. They shift a bit." As far as Lola knew, Janet had not had a memory incident in some time now. She had come to believe the situation had resolved itself, just as Janet had predicted.

"Can I tell you what happened?" Janet cried impatiently.

"I'm all ears."

Janet opened her mouth to begin but then started to cry instead, in earnest. Lola could see her scanning the table for something to wipe her face with. Fearing she might reach for one of the potholders, Lola jumped out of her chair and ripped a sheet of paper toweling from the roll on the counter. She handed it to her and sat again. "I had to pee," Janet wailed pathetically. "So I got up and walked to the bathroom. And, you know how they have that huge stone shower stall in the bathroom out there in the patio section?"

Lola nodded.

"Well, the glass door to the stall was open and I walked right it, into the shower, and I started to pull down my pants …"

"What do you mean?"

"What do you mean, *what do I mean?* I'm trying to tell you what I mean! I lost my mind! I was about to pee squatting there in the shower. Then I kind of snapped out of it. I was horrified! How could that happen to me?"

"Oh, Janet. That must have been terrible. But I don't think—"

Janet huffed, suddenly angry. "You're the one always busting me about memory loss. Here I'm trying to say you might be right, and you're poo-pooing my ... my incident."

Lola moved in closer, so that she could place her arm halfway across Janet's back. "Janet, I'm not poo-pooing you, really. But you have to factor in that you were high. Maybe you shouldn't get high when you go to Lynnie's house. It's not like you're used to smoking all the time. And she's always got such strong stuff. We're not kids anymore, you know."

Janet rolled her eyes. "That's for sure. I tell you, it was awful. I saw myself as someone else would have seen me if the bathroom door had been open. An old fat boring woman with Alzheimer's mistaking the shower stall for the toilet. I walked in there with a totally empty mind. Now I know what dementia feels like."

"But then you snapped out of it."

"But what if it happens again? What if that was a precursor? What if I'm *really* losing my mind? I'm all alone in the world, Lola. Who will take care of me?" She pushed her cup aside and put her arms on the table and her head on her arms and began to sob.

Lola scooted sideways until her chair was right alongside of Janet's, touching it. She wrapped both her arms around her and tried to rock her sideways, though it was awkward in that position. "You're overreacting, honey. This incident you're describing sounds like something that could have easily happened to a twenty-year-old partying too hard. It doesn't feel related to memory. But a twenty-year-old would have come out of the bathroom laughing, saying to her friends, *You'll never guess what I almost did.* Everyone would have laughed."

"You don't understand," Janet sniveled, and she began to sob harder.

Lola spoke loudly, to be heard over all the noise she was making. "We'll make an appointment then. We'll go to a doctor. Together."

Janet calmed down and eventually lifted her head. "You would do that?" she squeaked.

"Yes, I promise. We will do it together."

Janet thought for a minute. "How come you're so nice to me lately?"

Lola tilted her head. She'd been wondering herself. "Maybe I had an epiphany. Maybe some part of me that was angry about … well, everything, just broke off and flew away." She freed one hand to make a shooing gesture.

For a while Janet just looked at her. Then she said, "*We should always keep on nodding terms with the people we used to be, whether they were good company or not.* You ever hear that before?" She broke into a huge grin. "That's Joan Didion! From the book about Bethlehem. I just remembered it because I liked it when I read it. I always thought that was sage advice."

"That's amazing!" Lola cried. "I read the book too but I didn't recognize the quote. You're amazing! You see? What a memory!"

"Thank you," Janet mumbled, her pink face glowing now beneath its glaze of tears.

Lola pulled Janet toward her and kissed her cheek, three loud smacks like she used to give Valerie when she was upset about something. In response, and as if suddenly terribly embarrassed, Janet swung her head away. "What the hell is going on there?" she grumbled, noticing the orange paint for the first time."

Lola laughed. "The orange is only the background."

"Oh my god, Lolo. And here I'm worrying about *my* mind."

"I'm going full-out Bhil."

"Bhil?"

"Remember when I painted the hutch I told you about a fairytale where everyone painted their houses bright colors so it would rain? Well, the story originates with a tribe somewhere in India. I did some research and discovered it. Online. Legend has it that in ancient times they suffered a catastrophic drought, so they sought out a shaman and he told them they should paint their houses and rain would come. They painted everything, inside and out, using lots of bright colors and designs with lots of dots in them. And rain came." She shrugged. "Of course they didn't just paint dots. They painted trees and flowers and people and animals with dot designs inside them. I can't draw, so I can't do that. But I can do dots. I think."

Janet rolled her eyes. "Oh, for Pete's sake, find me a brush."

"No, you're going to help?"

"Why not? I'll never be crazy enough to ruin my own furniture, but maybe if the gods see me helping you ruin yours, they'll cut me some slack. I could use a little rain myself." She chuckled. "I bet people back east would never say such a thing. You have to live in a desert to understand, right?"

Later, after they'd painted numerous blue dots (tomorrow Lola would paint the yellows) in the areas Lola had designated with her roll of tape, Lola made avocado and tomato sandwiches and told Janet all about the unplanned breakfast she'd had with Rosa Hernandez and her granddaughter and the polished rock Rosa had given her. "I bought a gift for the kid, Karen, a charm for her bracelet," she said. "I wanted so badly for them to like me. I'd probably have given them Blue if I thought they'd take him. Or maybe even Pete. I so wanted to express … I don't know … some solidarity with them, because of Jamie's death. But I didn't even get to mention Jamie. The conversation just didn't go that way. And then I didn't give Karen the charm either! I left in the car and forgot all about it until I was halfway down the street. I turned back, but I didn't want to knock again so I put it in their mailbox." She drifted off, picturing the gift box, wrapped in chalk blue paper with darker blue ribbons, sitting alone in the mounted mailbox at the edge of the road. "But wait, I'll show you the rock."

Lola jumped up from her chair and hurried out of the room and returned with the green stone sitting in the middle of her palm. "I guess Rosa Hernandez wanted me to have something of hers."

"Why would you think that?" Janet asked, lifting the pretty stone from her hand.

"What do you mean?"

"It was probably his, Jamie's. She probably wanted you to have something of *his*. So you see, they gave you what they thought you needed anyway, *without* you having to ask."

Lola's mouth fell open. She hadn't even considered that.

"But the charm," Janet continued. "Did you at least have a card attached to it?"

"No, I didn't even know the kid's name until I got there."

"How will she know it's from you? I doubt they checked for mail yesterday, on a Sunday. By the time they look and see it today … Or maybe they won't look until tomorrow, who knows? They'll be scratching their heads with the possibilities. They might think it's from you or they might think it's some boy the girl has a crush on."

"Oh my," Lola marveled. "I hadn't thought of that."

"You're missing the obvious, on two counts now," Janet said smugly.

"Says the woman who mistook a shower stall for a toilet," Lola quipped, and they both had a good laugh.

12

BEN
surrender

Ben had finished breakfast in the shelter and was outside with Nancy, who'd watched Siggy while he ate. He'd officially offered her the stolen blanket earlier in the week, on the condition that she let Siggy spend nights in her car *temporarily*. He hadn't indicated how long he hoped that might be and she hadn't asked. All he knew was that nights were getting cooler. In fact, just the night before had been quite cold. There were several small parks a short walking distance from the shelter, and he'd been sleeping in one or another of them, but no matter how close he got to shrubs and trees, he hadn't found a place where he didn't feel out in the open, vulnerable. He didn't want Siggy exposed like that.

But *temporarily* was an ambiguous word, and it was only a matter of time before Nancy decided enough was enough. She was losing patience already. A couple times she got to the shelter before Ben in the morning and was annoyed that she'd had to wait a minute or two for him to show up and then wait for him to eat too so she could get on with her day. She still had his garbage bag in her trunk. She'd told him just the day before that she hoped he'd find another place for it sooner than later. Someone had offered to give her a fire extinguisher and she'd had to refuse it because her trunk was overfull. "Why would you need a fire extinguisher anyway?" he'd asked her.

She'd looked him in the eye. "Same reason you needed a down comforter, honey."

He nodded and looked at his feet. "Stupid question."

Nancy was about to cross the street and drive off when an elderly woman pulled up right beside where they were standing in what looked to be an extremely well-maintained antique—maybe 1985—Buick LaSabre, brown lower body with a wheat-colored roof, a classic. Nancy's mouth dropped open at the sight of it and she immediately turned to face the brick wall she'd been leaning against. The woman got out, locked her door with her key, and walked right past Nancy and Ben, to the front door of the shelter. After she entered, Nancy turned to Ben. "Oh my God, that was Mrs. Quick! I hope she didn't see me or recognize my car. What can she be doing here?"

"Mrs. *Who?*"

"The old lady who lets me park in her driveway every night!" she barked.

"Why didn't you want her to see you?"

"I don't want her to see me *here*. I don't want her to know my business. I don't want her to think I come to the shelter to eat most days. I want her to think I'm doing better, that the day might come when I won't have to sleep in her driveway."

Ben shrugged. "But she must realize—"

"That's not the point," Nancy snapped. "I'm doomed if she decides to kick me out before I'm ready to go. What do you *not* understand, Ben? She's the only security I have in this life. Go in. Please. Go in and see if you can figure out why she's here." Ben looked down at the carrier. "Go," she cried. "I'll stay here with him! You think I'd just leave him?"

Ben lingered a beat longer, mesmerized by her scowl; he wasn't sure he'd ever seen it so well defined before. It truly marred her beautiful face. He found it hard to believe he'd felt so close to her not that long ago.

He turned and walked into the shelter and went directly to the coffee counter. He could see the old woman, Mrs. Quick, talking to Frank, the guy who ran the place, over in the corner, outside Frank's office. She was all done up, with dangling earrings and what were probably pearls at her neck, wearing a powder blue pants suit with a silky looking cream-colored blouse beneath it. Her short grey hair was thick and curly; it might have been a wig. She was wearing black-framed glasses with a retainer chain. Her face was soft and pleasant-looking.

All the tables nearest them were full; there was no way he would be able to get close enough to hear what they were saying. But he sensed they were discussing them, the down-and-outers, because they were standing side by side, looking out at the sea of forlorn diners as they chatted. He poured some coffee into a Styrofoam cup and went outside again. "She's talking to Frank. I couldn't get close enough to hear," he told Nancy. "I doubt it has anything to do with you, if that's what you're worried about."

He spent the day walking around town with Siggy. Sometimes he took him out of the carrier and held him up on his chest. When his arm got tired, he put him back in and talked a little louder, so Siggy could still hear him. He tried to explain why it was necessary for Siggy to spend nights in a car, with someone who probably didn't say a kind word to him. He didn't bother mentioning that the arrangement was only temporary and that things would likely get worse before they got better. He tried not let his mind wander to the freezing cold nights that winter would bring, in case Siggy was reading his thoughts.

He may have looked like a crazy man walking around whispering to his big gray cat, but he and Siggy were actually on a mission. They were scoping out neighborhoods, like two criminals. They were looking for houses listed for sale, houses that appeared to be already vacated. Ben was thinking that if Nancy threw Siggy out of her car before he had a new plan, they could spend some nights in a garage, or even a shed behind an empty house if they could find a way to break in. Or even a carport could work for a while.

It was trash day, so they were also watching for offerings that might entice Nancy to keep Siggy with her nights a little longer, and also to keep Ben's trash bag safe in her trunk: scrap metal, Mason jars or old perfume bottles, anything Nancy might conclude had some value. It would be impossible to walk around with all his stuff day after day. He'd have to set up in one of the parks and then stay put to keep everything from being stolen. How would he eat? He'd need to make friends, people he could trust. How was that possible in a world where no one trusted anyone? He knew from other down-and-outers that most folks weren't bothered so much by the sight of one homeless person hanging out in the park, or even two, but once they sensed that the numbers were growing, that a community might be forming, they felt threatened and called the police and then everybody had to split up and go their separate ways. Eventually he'd have to find a tent, or fashion a make-shift one out of plastic bags and grocery carts. The orange and white roadblock loomed ahead, possibly closer than ever.

If he'd had a phone, he might have called Ruthie and asked her to consider taking Siggy back, for Siggy's sake, so he would not have to endure a winter without a roof over his head. Although the house was on the other side of town, some twenty miles away, he could have walked there and asked in person, but he couldn't bear the shame of having Ruthie and Moon see him as he was now—dirty, stinking, wearing all the same clothes he'd been wearing since the morning he'd awoken in the hotel room, his ripped jeans held together by a length of red duct tape (matching the one on Siggy's carrier; it was all Frank had), all so as not to have to inconvenience Nancy by asking her to let him get some clean stuff out of his bag before it was absolutely necessary. *Swindled, humiliated, hopeless.*

For all he knew, he had tetanus. He couldn't remember when he had his last shot. Probably in high school, or maybe even grade school. He remembered a camp counselor once explaining how serious tetanus could be, how you got lockjaw first, and then spasms in your neck muscles. Then you couldn't swallow. And eventually your legs and arms went rigid. When the counselor left Ben and his six or seven campmates that night, the boys had a fine time faking tetanus, throwing themselves on the cabin floor, stiffening their limbs, letting their tongues roll out of their mouths. In his mind's eye Ben saw the pigeon dangling by its wing from the razor wire. Dead or alive, he couldn't say. He only knew the thing was still. How he must have suffered to attain stillness. How he must have struggled. But stillness was possible; it lay just beyond the roadblock.

That evening he got to the shelter at the designated time and had to wait a full hour for Nancy to show up. Then he waited another half hour for her to eat. She came out with scraps for Siggy, though, and he quickly forgave her. "I've got news," she said, bending to lift Siggy's bowl out of the carrier pocket. She knew the rules. He had to admire her for that. She opened the carrier door and immediately attached the end of Siggy's leash to the carrier handle. Siggy looked at the food, then at Ben. *Do I have to?* he seemed to be asking. For a moment Ben worried he wouldn't, that he was getting sick, that he would pass on very soon and Ben would be alone in the world and the roadblock would pop up right there in front of him. But then Siggy began to eat. A second wave of gratitude washed over him. He closed his eyes. *The little things*, he thought. Why had he never realized before? He'd had so many of them throughout his life and he'd never once realized.

Nancy straightened. She looked again like her perky self, the one he had half fallen in love with, if only briefly, that night out on the ledge. "So, Mrs. Quick, the old lady from this morning? She's clearing a section of her land. That's why she was here. She's got a thing for homeless people, don't you know. She's going to hire people from the shelter to work for her—"

Ben's mouth dropped open with joy, but Nancy put her hand up. "Wait wait wait, not so fast, mister," she warned. "She told Frank she would only take men who have never been in trouble with the law. That leaves you out, buddy. But after the land is cleared, she's going to want a contractor be-cause she's going to build some tiny houses. I like tiny houses. I think they're so cute. Anyway, maybe you can somehow clear it with her by then."

"Tiny houses for who?"

"Beats me. Frank told that guy Norman, the big guy with the red bandana and all the tats? And Norman told Ceil and Ceil told me. Just now. I'm only hoping it won't impinge on my needs. I'll have to be sure to be gone from her driveway every morning before any work starts and stay out long enough for any work vehicles she has there to leave at the end of the day. I don't know what's going to happen. I don't know when either. All I know is that's what she came to the shelter to talk to Frank about."

"You think she'd let me at least talk to her?"

"No, I don't, Ben. That's one thing Ceil made clear. She said Norman said that Frank said he's going to have to vet everyone, the hard way, by calling the police department, and anyone who's got a record of any sort is out. O.U.T."

"You going there now? To Mrs. Quick's driveway for the night?"

"Yep. It's that time. Where else would I go?"

"Take me with you."

Nancy scoffed. "You can't be serious! Do you not give a shit at all what happens to me?"

"I do, Nancy, I do." He thought a minute. "How about you drive me close by and drop me off and you go park in her driveway as always, and I'll just show up, independent of you. She'll never know you had anything to do with it. I'll say I heard about her wanting to hire and walked over. She'll never even know we know each other."

Nancy nodded angrily. "Sure, Ben, sure. Unless she happened to see us this morning, standing here with your *cat*."

He didn't like the way she'd referred to Siggy, with disdain. "She can't have seen you. You were facing the building before she even got out of her car."

Nancy held out a strand of her hair, which was platinum blond. "You think she didn't see this? I'm a little hard to miss, wouldn't you say?" She let go of the lock but it stayed where she'd pulled it, as if it was made of cotton candy.

"She didn't even look our way."

"No, Ben. The answer is *no*. I'm not going to give you the chance to wreck *my* life."

Her emphasis on *my* made him gasp. It implied a pattern of wreckage. He took a deep breath and looked at his feet. It would do him no good at all to react to her meanness. "Where does she live?" he mumbled.

She laughed. "You think I'm going to tell you?"

No, he didn't. But he had to try. "Okay," he conceded. He picked up Siggy, who had finished eating by then, and the two rubbed their heads together, communicating in their special language what had to be communicated before they parted for the night. Ben kissed Siggy's nose and tucked him gently into his carrier. He dusted off his bowl and replaced it in the carrier pocket. "See you in the morning," he said to Nancy. "I'm very grateful," he added, "for all you do for me. Maybe I don't say that enough."

She took the carrier from him and crossed the street to her car.

Ben sat at a table with three other men, all of them ten or more years his junior. "You guys hear some lady in town is looking for bums like us to clear her land?" he asked.

That was all it took to get things started. Everyone had heard something, and so while Ben worked on his dinner—fries, hamburger with onions, no buns; they must have run out before he got inside—his table mates put the story together. Two of the three men had a prison record, so for them the gossip was only that. But one was thinking he might apply. He said he'd heard Frank was going to make an announcement the next day and then the old lady was coming back the day after or the one after that and whoever wanted to apply would have the chance to interview with her. "It's all the ways out there," the guy lamented, "ten, fifteen miles, somewhere west of 2nd and north of Osuna."

"I know that area," Ben said. "What street?"

"Sunshine Vista? Vista Sunshine? Something like that. How the hell is anyone going to get out there every day to work? Fly?"

Ben finished his meal and gulped down his water. The guy had gotten it wrong. It was Sunshine Visa, not Vista. Moon had had a friend in that neighborhood when she was a little girl. He'd driven her to a birthday party out there one time. And once he'd taken her to the same house to do a school project with the same girl. He had all the information he needed.

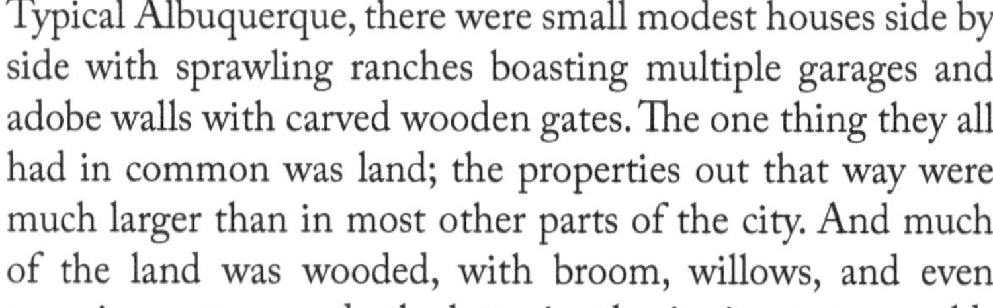

Typical Albuquerque, there were small modest houses side by side with sprawling ranches boasting multiple garages and adobe walls with carved wooden gates. The one thing they all had in common was land; the properties out that way were much larger than in most other parts of the city. And much of the land was wooded, with broom, willows, and even towering cottonwoods, the latter just beginning to turn gold.

It had taken him three hours to walk there—and he only found the place because Nancy's Jetta was in the driveway.

Mrs. Quick's place had to be a double- or triple-sized lot, because it was even bigger than the others in the area—a great property with lots of trees and shrubs and a sizable vegetable garden surrounded by a chain-link fence. The house was a wooden farmhouse, old and dilapidated, as were the detached garage and the two sheds he could see from the street.

He planned to wait until morning to knock. It was already dark, and he'd have to wait for Nancy to vacate the driveway anyway. Who knew what she'd do if she spotted him. The problem was that when she left, she'd be heading to the shelter to meet him, to drop off Siggy. What would happen when he didn't show up? How long would she wait? He heard the echo of what she'd said when she'd sent him inside to spy on Frank and Mrs. Quick. *You think I'd just leave him?* No, she'd be furious with Ben, and she'd have to put Siggy back in the car and drive around with him all day, but she wouldn't leave him out on the road. *That* she wouldn't do. Homeless people became hopeless people, and hopeless people lost their humanity over time. They did things they'd never have imagined themselves capable of. But Nancy wasn't there yet. She had a car and a driveway to park it in and bathroom facilities in one of the sheds. She still had some hope.

He found a place to sleep on Mrs. Quick's property, behind the larger of the two wooden sheds, under some cottonwood trees and well away from the door. But while the prospect of Nancy abandoning Siggy seemed all but impossible only a short time before, as soon as he zipped himself up in his sleeping bag, it became absolutely conceivable. The moon appeared and the wind picked up, and his mind went in circles, spinning out one worst-case scenario after another.

There was a shallow creek out amid the cottonwoods. Ben climbed down the embankment in the morning and washed his face and hands with a sliver of soap he'd found in a gas station men's room the day before. He pulled his jeans down to his ankles and had a good look at his leg. The cut wasn't healed; the skin had not closed over it. But the leg itself didn't appear to be infected.

He used the last of the soap to wash the wound. Then he walked back up and waited behind a cholla patch until he saw Nancy back out of the driveway. He sat for a half hour longer, listening to the wind—which had to be blowing at twenty-five miles per hour or more, from the south—picturing Nancy outside the shelter with Siggy in his carrier at her feet, looking down the street, watching for him to appear, her lips pressed together hard, her hand near her face to keep her cotton candy hair from flying into it.

He walked out to the street under the cover of trees and shrubs and then walked up the driveway and rang the bell.

He took a deep breath. This was it. This was his one chance.

The old lady opened the front door but left the security door, which was covered in aluminum privacy mesh, in place. He couldn't really see her through it. "Mrs. Quick?" he said to her silhouette.

"No solicitors," she croaked.

He cleared his throat. "I'm not really soliciting," he said. "I'm currently without a home, for reasons that would make sense if I could explain them. I need work badly. I'm an architect. I've worked on lots of projects in town. I might even be able to get some references. You need to build houses and I know how to do it. You need someone to design them, from the ground up. But first you have to clear the land, get things ready. I'm your man. I can organize crews. I can tell them exactly what to do and when to do it. I can work alongside them."

He realized he was talking over her.

"—interviews in a couple of days," he heard her say.

"I can handle everything from start to finish," he went on quickly. "I have the exact right credentials. I was in jail, but only a couple of days. Wrongly accused, so it doesn't count."

"No," she said in her quiet voice. "I told Frank I don't want anyone who's been in that kind of trouble. Now you'll have to leave, please."

"Please, Mrs. Quick. Please. I'm the exact person you need to handle this. You've got to understand how it works, the groundbreaking, the footers and foundations, the rough framing, the rough plumbing and electrical and HVAC. Insulation, drywall, when to call the building inspector, where to get the best supplies and how much in advance to order them. How to get the best price. You can't just start without knowing what steps to follow and in what sequence. I don't even want any money. Just some food. I can sleep in the shed."

"No," she said. "Please don't come back here, all right?"

"Please, Mrs. Quick. Please just hear me out. Please. I'm begging you."

"I'm going to shut the door now," she said. And she did. She shut it slowly, quietly. Ben heard the click when the latch caught, and a second click when she turned the lock.

"I have a cat," he went on, speaking a little louder. He doubted she could hear him, even if she was still standing there. But he wasn't so much talking to her anymore as he was to the universe. "He's old and he'll die if I don't find shelter for him over the winter." He stared at his feet. His sneakers were filthy and the right one had a small hole where his big toe would soon poke through.

"I was in the wrong place at the wrong time. My wife and I had an argument, over something really stupid …" He hesitated, remembering.

"Really stupid," he mumbled.

His old college friend had texted that he was on a road trip, heading to California from the East Coast with his new girlfriend. His wife, who had been Ben's friend too way back when, had died the year before. He would be in Albuquerque the next evening, and he wanted to know what hotel Ben would recommend. Ben texted back that they were welcome to stay at his place.

Ruthie had never met Charlie but she wanted to make him feel welcomed too. She was like that. Warmhearted. She went through her cookbooks and found something to make and then ran out to the store and bought all the ingredients, and stuff for appetizers and a couple of different desserts, a couple bottles of wine, and by the time they got to the house the next day she was all ready for them.

But when they walked in, and the girlfriend, Lois, who was so young she could have been Charlie's daughter, saw the table all set with plates and napkins and a vase of fresh flowers, her face fell. She mumbled something about how they'd passed a few restaurants on their way over and she'd been hoping they could all go out to eat. Charlie tried to laugh it off. *Oh, come on, honey. This will be fun. We can get New Mexican on our way back home.*

Lois sat down and basically pushed her food around her plate, trying to get the peppers and eggplant off to the side, because, she said, *nightshades cause cancer.* That put a damper on the conversation. Charlie and Ben tried to bring up some of the funny incidents that happened back in college, but each time the girlfriend would sigh or roll her eyes. Ruthie asked her what she thought of Albuquerque driving in and she said something like, *I had hoped we'd see more by going out for dinner,* and Ruthie responded, *Well, you'll see more tomorrow, heading back to the interstate,* and the girlfriend scoffed and said, *We'll be in a hurry to get on the road then. I think the window of opportunity for sightseeing has closed for us.*

That last bit was what did it. Ruthie made them breakfast in the morning, but she could barely look at them. When they left, she and Ben had the fight. She blamed him for having a friend who would want to be with a woman like Lois. Ben tried to say that Charlie wasn't like that back in the old days, but Ruthie reminded him of some stories he had told her that proved otherwise. Charlie was shallow, she said, and so was Ben.

"Stupid," Ben said to Mrs. Quick's door. "Stupid, stupid, stupid. So I went to a bar that night. I never went to bars.

"Gino's. There was only one empty seat. Turned out the people who were there, all men, were having a bachelor party. I took the seat, and probably because they were all drunk to begin with, no one seemed to realize I wasn't one of the guests, and one or another of them kept buying drinks for everyone sitting there, including me, and I wound up drinking way more than I would have otherwise. Bunch of young rednecks. They must have thought I was the bride's great uncle or something. One even clapped me on the back when he got to the punch line of some joke he was telling. And they had this woman come in to … you know, to dance around, get up on the bar and tease. And this one guy tried to grab her and this other guy, I think it was the one the party was for, the groom, punched him.

"A bunch of drunk men. A brawl. I shouldn't have been there. It got out of hand fast and soon everyone was punching everyone. I was just sitting there—I swear it on my grave—just sitting there, stunned, and drunk, I admit, and someone hit me over the head with a bottle.

"All I wanted was to go home, tell Ruthie I was sorry. But the blood … I was dizzy. I couldn't even get up. There were sirens. Everyone was getting out of there. Except me. And this one other guy, but he wasn't moving."

Ben bent his head against the security door and began to cry softly. It occurred to him that Mrs. Quick might have called the police, that any minute he would hear sirens. They'd probably put him in jail again. He didn't really care.

"And then … and then … All these other things I did wrong over the years. My wife, she couldn't help stringing them all together. It was like she was building a train. The incident in the bar was the engine, and all these other things, some of which I didn't even remember, none of which were that bad, were getting hitched to it. She said she couldn't help it.

"We went to a therapist, but that did no good. Instead of telling Ruthie she had to disconnect all the cars and just deal with the engine, the woman said it was understandable, that that's how the human mind works when it's assaulted with too much pain. I didn't defend myself. I let the two of them do all the talking that first visit, because I thought it would help. I figured I'd get my chance next time. But there was no next time. Ruthie felt validated. She didn't need to go back. And a few days later she said she couldn't stand the sight of me." Ben took a deep breath to keep from sobbing again.

"And my daughter. My daughter, my Moon … I was living in the spare room by then, through the trial. She must have thought of me as a boarder, an intruder. I'm living in this nightmare, lawyer one day, court the next. I'm praying daily that the truth will come out and I won't spend the rest of my life in prison for something I didn't do. I was losing my mind. A couple of the other witnesses remembered seeing me there, accepting drinks that came my way. But in the end, no one could remember me throwing a single punch. My blood was found only on myself, on my own clothing. And no one else's blood was found on me. Two lawyers got rich on my stupidity—and eight months later I was finally declared innocent.

"I didn't work all that time. I even sold my work truck, which was practically new, in case I needed quick cash. Even though she'd said some terrible things to me, I hoped my innocence might change things and I asked Ruthie if I could move back into our room. And she said no. Very calm, busy at the sink; didn't even look at me. She said she'd met someone. That she felt it was the right thing to let me stay until the trial was over. But now that I was a free man, she wanted me out."

Ben was suddenly very tired, beyond tired, more tired than he ever remembered being in his entire life. "I left. An old friend said I could stay in his shed until I found work. Shed had its own bathroom. Back home I had to walk down the hall from the spare room to use my daughter's bathroom, and I knew she resented me for it. I figured I'd find a job quick and work on getting back in my daughter's good graces. But then COVID happened and everyone in construction was shutting down. I bought a hotplate, so I could heat up canned foods, and a secondhand TV. And then I just stayed in bed all day every day with the TV running. I lived like that for a while, like a hermit, until finally my friend told me it was time for me to get out of his shed and move on.

"I went to a cheap hotel. I got vaccinated. I started looking again. But when I still didn't find anything, I took up this young guy's offer to spend the summer sleeping out on a ledge under one of the overpasses along 40. Thought it might be good for me. That it would force me to pull myself together. I was sure I'd find something. I'd been a big deal in my field. But looking for work is a whole different story when you're living under an overpass. You can't keep your phone charged. You can't keep yourself clean. I spent most of my time walking back and forth between the ledge and the shelter. And now, with winter coming, I'm worried about my cat."

The dead pigeon popped into Ben's head just then, dangling from the barbed wire out on the ledge.

He let himself slide down along the side of the house. He landed hard on the stoop. He closed his eyes for a few minutes; he might have fallen asleep. When he opened them again, he found himself looking at the red duct tape on his knee. He didn't have tetanus after all; he knew that now. Too bad. It would have been quick. No one would have needed to take care of him. He looked out toward the street. He could see a small house up the hill from Mrs. Quick's property. It might have been the same one he'd driven Moon to years before. Across from it was a larger one, new looking, a high stucco wall surrounding it. A roadrunner appeared out of nowhere, not ten feet from where he sat. It stopped to look him over. It seemed to be interested in the tears bubbling up over his eyes. Moon loved roadrunners. When she saw one she always spoke to it. "Hello, Mr. Roadrunner," he mumbled.

"My daughter, Moon, her real name is Mona," he said to no one. He looked up at the sky. "The night everything happened, before I went out, she came into the living room and sat next to me. She said, *Mom's going through a rough patch. It'll be okay.* And she leaned her head on my shoulder and we just sat there, quietly."

It took all the willpower he had to stand again. "Well, Mrs. Quick," he said in a louder voice. "I don't blame you for not wanting anyone like me to work for you. I wouldn't hire me either. I'm a fool. I ruined not only my own miserable life but my wife's and my daughter's too."

He sobbed into his fist. He couldn't stop. "And truth is," he said when he could, "there are younger guys with their lives still all ahead of them. Younger, stronger … Guys who lost their jobs because of the pandemic, the economy, no fault of their own. Guys who never got in any kind of trouble with the law. Guys who wouldn't have been there in a place like Gino's in the first place. You did the right thing, telling Frank you only want guys who are clean. You did the right thing."

He took a step away from the door and then turned back. "Mrs. Quick, I'm thirsty." He hesitated for a moment, once again imagining Nancy arriving at the shelter this morning, waiting for him, giving up, putting Siggy back in her car and driving away. Or leaving Siggy behind, in his carrier. "I'm going to step away from the door, and I'm going to walk down along the side of your house here and turn on your faucet and drink from your hose. I just want you to know so you won't get scared when you hear the water go on. Unless you happen to have any bottled water. If you wanted to give me a bottle, I'd accept it with deep gratitude."

He waited another few minutes. Then he walked down the side of the house and turned on the spigot and drank from the hose. When he'd had his fill, he put the hose back as he'd found it and turned off the spigot. Then he got his sleeping bag and his backpack from the stoop and started the long walk back toward the shelter.

He walked bent over, half to keep blowing dust out of his eyes and half because he was struck down, a grown man whimpering, because he had a daughter who didn't love him and a cat he couldn't take care of. Because he had come to hate himself. Because he had been counting on the tetanus to do what he couldn't.

He had to walk through a busy intersection. He saw other homeless people there, none of whom he knew. He wouldn't this far out from his territory. Some had signs. Some had set themselves up on medians near stop lights. When traffic stopped they walked up and down, looking for someone to hand them a bill.

He had never done that. He had never begged. With the shelter so nearby, he had never had to. But as he was crossing the street a red sedan slowed down beside him and he heard a voice, and when he turned to look, he saw a little girl holding out a bill, a twenty. He stepped toward the car, speechless. He looked at the child through burning eyes. He looked at the mother, who was staring straight ahead, watching for the light to change. He wanted to ask her if she realized her kid was trying to give him a twenty. If Moon had done that, he would have told her *No, that's too much. That guy will only drink it away or use it to buy drugs. It will only encourage* ... But he couldn't get the words out. He waited for the bill to disappear but the girl only extended her arm further. Finally he took the money. The light changed. The car pulled away. He hadn't even said thank you.

The wind was still blowing that evening when he walked to the shelter from the nearby park where he'd spent the afternoon sleeping under a tree between two piles of dog shit. Nancy was there, with Siggy and his trash bag. As soon as she saw him coming, she crossed the street and marched to her car. He could see she was fuming. He called out her name, but she ignored him. By the time he reached the carrier, she was already pulling away. But he had his cat. He had Siggy.

There was a sleazy hotel down the street. A lot of the down-and-outers went there when they came into a little cash. Since the place was too run-down to attract business or tourist crowds, the owner was open to negotiations.

Ben got a room for $15.00, including tax. He dropped off his trash bag and backpack and sleeping bag. He hated to leave Siggy behind in a place like that, but he had no choice. He couldn't bring him into the shelter, and he couldn't count on there being someone who would stay with him outside in the wind. He picked him up and held him to his chest and explained that he had to have something to eat. Siggy purred.

Ben hustled back to the shelter. His dinner—baked ziti with watered-down tomato sauce—was the first thing he'd had all day. He gobbled it down and asked Dolly if he could have seconds. She looked around. The wind, which was really blowing by then, had kept some of the regulars away. She nodded and Ben went back for a refill.

Since Siggy couldn't eat ziti, he filled a Styrofoam cup with grated parmesan and stuffed it under his shirt, in the hollow where his belly had once been. He was about to pilfer a container of milk as well when Frank appeared. Ben froze. Frank could be a hard ass. He couldn't afford to lose his visitors' privilege. That would be the roadblock in itself, right there. But apparently Frank didn't notice the bulge in Ben's shirt. "You really an architect?" Frank asked.

"You didn't know that?" Ben replied nervously.

"You think I have the luxury of learning all the stories that go along with all you folks?"

"Why? Why you want to know that now?"

"You heard about old lady Quick? The one who wants to hire men to clear some land?"

Ben nodded.

"Said someone calling himself an architect made a nuisance of himself out there this morning. She described him and I figured it had to be you. That true? You make a nuisance of yourself? You pick up her garden hose and have yourself a drink like you owned the place?"

Ben nodded again. The Styrofoam cup under his shirt slipped sideways. He could feel the cheese morsels spreading out on his skin. "I can explain—"

"Explain to her, not me. She wants you there tomorrow, same time as today. You going to be able to manage that?"

"She wants me there because I was a nuisance?"

Frank shrugged. "I don't know why she wants you. Ain't my business, is it? All I know is she told me to tell you to come back. Same time." He turned, but then he turned back. He clapped his palm on Ben's bony shoulder. "Good luck, buddy, okay?" he said, and he walked away.

13

LOLA

nostos

Years before, Lola had purchased a barnwood farm-style coffee table from a local antique shop. In November she painted the tabletop dark red. Then Janet found a roll of brown packing paper and between the two of them they managed to draw the outline of an elephant standing beneath a couple of simplistic but thick-trunked Baobab trees. They cut out patterns and traced the outlines on the red tabletop and then filled in the shapes with dots and stripes in different colors. They liked the blue dots the best, so they used that same color for the table legs, which Lola had sanded down to rid them of Blue's teeth marks.

The table came out so good that Janet insisted they have Thanksgiving dinner at Lola's house that year, so everyone could see their artwork. Lola hadn't hosted a Thanksgiving dinner since before Valerie died and George—who was gone now too, having passed quietly in hospice in October—left her. She and Janet invited Lynnie and Fred and Sophie and Carol and their husbands and a handful of other friends and they had a party, replete with dancing, because Lynnie brought over some of her favorite CDs and insisted on it. She also brought over some weed, and Janet—who was no longer worried about memory loss, because she and Lola had been to two doctors and both had concluded that other than some age-related deterioration, her brain was functioning fine—smoked a great deal of it and was loud bordering on obnoxious, but also very funny. Everyone was in tears laughing at her stories.

In December, Lola and Janet created a table for Lynnie, who had fallen in love with their designs at Thanksgiving. She commissioned them to come up with a cat motif, and while they said they'd have been happy to do it just for fun, she insisted on paying them. That led them to research the Bhil people whose style was always their inspiration, and when they learned that they were mostly illiterate and often suffering from preventable diseases and malnutrition, they looked for organizations that advocated on their behalf. They found one that was working to build schools and hospitals to support the next generation of Bhil children. They sent them Lynnie's money, along with equal amounts of their own.

They spent New Year's Eve together, just the two of them, drinking champagne and making resolutions. One of them was that they would start hiking together, at least once a week. Lola had always loved hiking, but she didn't do much of it after George left. There were so many great trails up in the foothills of the Sandias, and if someone invited her she always said yes, but she had never cared to hike on her own. There were too many pitfalls—not only the prospect of rattlers, black bears, or cougars but also numerous places where you could twist an ankle climbing over rocks. It was a good idea to have a partner.

The first time they hiked together, along with Pete and Blue, Janet moaned the whole time because she couldn't keep up. But that week she lost two pounds, and then she couldn't wait to go again. Thereafter they pushed themselves each time to climb a little higher, go a little farther, and they returned home exhausted and exhilarated. Once they hiked just after a snow storm. There were some footprints, so people had already been on the trail they favored, but the hikers—it seemed there were only two of them—had to have come and gone because there hadn't been a single car in the lot when they arrived. They let the dogs off their leashes, and Pete and Blue ran back and forth like puppies, dipping their snouts into the snow and tossing their heads to throw it up in the air when they had to stop to wait for Janet and Lola to catch up. Sometimes when they hiked they could hear the sound of traffic in the distance, but on that day, it was dead quiet, and with the snow glinting in the sun, beautiful beyond words. On the way back, they found a mini-snowman on the trail, maybe ten inches high. He had stick arms and small stones for eyes. Lola wanted to take a picture, but before she could get her gloves off and her phone out of her backpack, Blue ran into him and his two upper segments rolled away. Lola tried to put him back together but the snowballs that were his torso and head iced over and wouldn't stick. Not long after, they spotted two snow angels side by side, one bigger than the other. A man and a woman. They were perfect; they really looked like angels. The people who had made the mini-snowman and the angels were lovers, Lola was certain. She couldn't take her eyes off their angel shapes. "Come on, Lola," Janet urged, "I'm cold. I want to go home now."

That same month they worked on Lola's end tables, barnwood like the coffee table, and her entertainment unit, which George had built back when they'd first moved to New Mexico. Janet loved her furniture just as it was, but in February they painted one wall in her dining room black and then used the packing paper to make a pattern of cottonwood trees, which they copied onto the wall, filling the trunks and branches with row after row of warm-colored dots.

Their neighbor, Mrs. Quick, heard about their work from another neighbor and asked if she could come up and see for herself. She loved what Lola had done in her house, so they took her across the street to Janet's, and she loved the mural too. She asked them if they would paint one wall in each of the five tiny houses she was having built. She thought it would be fun to have a different design in each one, or at least different colors. They would have plenty of time to come up with ideas too, because the first of the houses was still some months from completion. In the meantime, Mrs. Quick suggested they meet once a week to discuss the designs they were considering.

She visited for two hours that day, and while the first twenty minutes were spent looking at and talking about Bhil, the rest of the time Mrs. Quick talked a blue streak, about her project mostly, the houses she was building at the back of her property, how the homeless men and women who were working for her so appreciated what she was doing for them, how they loved it when she came out with a tray of her signature cupcakes (Lola and Janet exchanged a quick look but managed not to laugh), how they were all so polite and how their stories were all so interesting that she thought she might even write a book about them one day, if she lived long enough. "Of course I won't use their real names," she said. "Some of their stories would knock your socks off."

After she left, Lola and Janet conceded that it wouldn't kill them to meet with her every week, though it was completely unnecessary as far as the designs were concerned;

it took them about five minutes to agree that they would stick with tree murals, five different species for each of the houses: aspens, desert willows, a honey mesquite, an Arizona Ash, and a Royal Poinciana with big red blossoms. Clearly, Mrs. Quick was lonely. That's why she talked so much. Probably that was why she'd started the construction project in the first place. She couldn't rent the tiny houses, she'd said, because her property was not zoned for that. But she planned to offer them to various homeless people who were trying to work their way *out* of homelessness. Lola and Janet bet that the homeless people who were the best listeners would have the greatest chance of scoring one of her rent-free properties. And feigning to love her cupcakes wouldn't hurt either.

In April, Mrs. Quick called Lola to say a cat belonging to one of her workers had passed on over the rainbow. When she told him that she didn't want any dead animals buried on her property but that the neighbor up the hill had a bona fide pet cemetery, he asked if Mrs. Quick would call and see if it was okay for him to bring the cat up.

Lola's first impulse was to tell Mrs. Quick that she would appreciate it if she didn't go around telling people she had a pet cemetery, that really it was only for *her* animals, and those of a few friends. And *why* couldn't the guy bury the cat on her property anyway? Certainly she had enough of it. Even after the huge space that had been cleared for the five tiny houses, there remained plenty more, back where the cotton-woods grew. But then she got to thinking that maybe Mrs. Quick had some kind of superstition about dead animals near her house. The more she and Janet got to know her, the nuttier she was revealed to be. Only a few days before she'd been up to Lola's and she'd gone on a rampage about food that was yellow. She swore she couldn't be in the same room with a jar of mustard. Lola had been preparing mustard and cheese sandwiches for their lunch when the subject came up and she'd had to put the mustard away and switch to guacamole.

Lola sighed, loudly she hoped, and asked if she needed to be there when the fellow came up with his cat. "No, not at all," Mrs. Quick said. "We can see the top of your shed from down here. I told him the cemetery is just beyond it. I imagine he'll be up sometime in the next hour or so."

"Fine," Lola said, "because I have things to do. I have to go out. Please ask him to be aware of the other sites. They're all marked, so it shouldn't be a problem. He'll need to mark his too somehow. There's a shovel out there, leaning against the shed. He can use that. Tell him to put it back where he got it when he's all done. And tell him to please dig the hole deep enough, at least three feet, and to wrap his cat properly."

"He knows all that, dear. He's an architect."

Lola had a training session with some new employees at Dog Planet that afternoon. Afterwards she stopped for groceries. She and some friends, Janet included, had begun meeting at one another's houses monthly for the purpose of discussing what was going on in the world and in what small ways they could help to remedy specific situations. They were already working with various churches that provided basic services for immigrants arriving in the area; and twice they had gone *en masse* to donate blood. Those who felt qualified—Lola, Janet, and one other woman—were pitching in at the new grief center. And at Lola's behest, someone from the local ASPCA was coming to talk to them about opportunities to support animal shelters.

Tonight was Lola's turn to host. As such, she would also be responsible for providing a meal. They had all—the group had started out with five women and was now at eleven women and one man—agreed that meals should be kept simple, to ensure they didn't forget the purpose of their meetings. Lola planned to make a cold pasta salad, served with garlic bread.

She was just putting away a box of rotini when she noticed from her kitchen window a head pop up over the hill that led down to Mrs. Quick's property. She had forgotten about the man coming up to bury his cat. She wondered why he had waited so long. She wondered if he had spent the whole day sitting with his dead cat or if he had wrapped him in a blanket and gone back to work and only just now remembered he had a cat to bury. She felt annoyed all over again. *Don't judge*, she told herself.

She stepped to the side so as not to be seen and watched him materialize incrementally—his shoulders, then his torso, then his legs. The sun was low in the sky behind him, and he almost seemed to shimmer mirage-like in the dusky yellow light. Once, when she and George and Valerie had vacationed in Maine, they'd watched a replica of a seventeenth-century galleon pass from Penobscot Bay to where they had gathered with a dozen or so other tourists, on the tip of the Phippsburg Peninsula. A ship that size, under full sail with her multiple decks and pine masts and prominent bulkhead, would have been a majestic sight in any circumstance. But on that particular day there was a heavy fog. The crowd stared into it, into the gray nothingness, for a long time. Then the shape of the ship began to define itself, a slightly darker gray that slowly materialized into the grand galleon, a representation of another time and place. It took their breath away to see it emerge like that, incrementally. Valerie, who'd always been so sensitive to things of beauty, had burst into tears of joy.

You would have expected a man who was burying a cat to carry him up in a box, but this man, the architect, carried his cat in his arms, in front of him, like a sacrifice. And he was wearing a suit for the occasion. It might have fit him well once, but now it was baggy, almost comically so. Maybe Mrs. Quick had loaned it to him, from whatever was left behind from her long deceased husband's wardrobe. In either case, it was somewhat wrinkled.

He had been walking straight toward her coming up over the hill but now he turned to the right, toward her shed, and made his way to the cemetery. She noticed he was wearing a backpack. She ran to the storage pantry, which had a small curtain-covered window. She parted the panels just enough to be able to see.

He'd reached the cemetery; he'd opened the gate and was looking around, deciding where. When he found the place he wanted—toward the back, so as not to be intrusive, she surmised—he placed his cat on the ground, gently, as if he were only asleep and he didn't want to wake him. He looked up, saw the shovel leaning against the shed.

He took his time—digging slowly, moving around the hole as he went. Every now and then he looked toward the path he'd taken up from Mrs. Quick's. When he was done digging, he removed his backpack and got down on his knees. From the pack he pulled forth a black plastic leaf bag, a small blanket of some sort, a towel, a little wooden box, and something else, small, maybe a kitty toy. He placed the towel beside him and the blanket, which he'd opened, in front of him. He lifted his cat to the center of the blanket, along with the toy, and folded it over him. Then he slipped the cat into the plastic bag, which he must have cut ahead of time so that it wouldn't be too deep. Again he looked back toward the path. Then he stretched back to look at the sky and bent forward again. Lola could tell he was crying because his too big jacket rose and fell along his shoulders and upper back.

Eventually he stilled. He looked back once more and this time he seemed to be smiling, a closed-lip sad smile. Then someone was coming into Lola's field of vision. A young woman. That's who he had smiled at. That's who he'd been waiting for. A young woman in tight jeans and a baby blue hoodie. She came through the gate and knelt down on the towel the architect had set out for her. They knelt side by side like that for a long time. Then he bent to lift the bag holding his cat and placed it in the ground. The young woman leaned her head on his shoulder. She put her arm around his back. They seemed to be crying together now. Lola found herself with tears in her eyes too.

The architect opened the wooden box and poked around at whatever was in it. Were they his keepsakes or the cat's? she wondered. She thought of the box Rosa Hernandez had brought to the table that day, the green stone that had belonged, most likely, to her son. *Love me, love my child*, Lola thought. That's what Rosa Hernandez had been saying. She understood that now. And in some strange way Lola did love Rosa Hernandez's child. Because Rosa had loved him. He had strayed. So had Valerie. What was different was the paths they chose to wander away on.

The architect selected something from the box, something small, another polished stone for all she knew, and held it up for the young woman's consideration. She nodded in agreement. He placed it into the grave.

Eventually the architect and the young woman got to their feet, and he began to fill in the hole while she watched. When he was done, they tamped the ground down together to even it out. He returned the shovel to where he'd found it. Then he gathered some broken branches and brought them back to the gravesite and pulled something from his pocket—cord, it had to be—and fashioned a marker, a cross. He drove it into the ground and then placed the wooden box at its foot. The young woman stood beside him, close, and he put his arm around her. They stood for a few minutes looking at the site. Then the architect picked up the box and put it in his backpack and put the pack on his shoulders. They started back toward the path that led down the hill to Mrs. Quick's place.

Lola shimmied herself out through the side door, so that the dogs, who had heard the door open and were already running in her direction, wouldn't try to follow. They were just going by, the architect with his arm still around the young woman, both of them walking with their heads down. She nearly ran into them.

"Oh," the architect exclaimed softly, jumping back. He looked toward the cemetery, pointed his thumb. "Is it okay?" he asked. "Mrs. Quick said …"

The sky was just beginning to darken. Lola got closer, so he could see her face. "It's fine," she said. "I didn't mean to scare you. I just wanted to let you know that you can visit whenever you want." She realized her mistake and covered her mouth with her fingertips. "Oh, dear. I meant your cat. You can visit your cat, the grave."

"Thank you."

"We've met before," she blurted, because she still wasn't sure he'd recognized her.

Before he could answer, the young woman stepped toward her. "You're Valerie's mother!" Her voice was full of wonderment. "I'm Mona. Do you remember me, maybe? I came by once to work on a project with her. I think we were drawing the planets."

Lola gulped back a sob against the back of her wrist. *Valerie's mother.* No one had called her that in a very long time. Mona reached out and embraced her.

The architect approached too, his face knotted in concern. "Are you all right?"

Mona released her and smiled warmly. Lola smiled back at her. Such a confident child. Valerie hadn't been like that. She reached out with a trembling hand and touched the side of Mona's face, pushing her hair back a little. "Yes," she said, still looking at Mona. "I'm fine." She laughed a little and looked at the architect. "I'm sorry. I didn't mean to hijack your ceremony with one of my own. I just wanted to say hello, and that you could visit."

"We would like that," Mona said.

The architect, who was standing behind his daughter, winked. "We would," he added.

Lola watched Ben take his daughter's hand. They started toward the path that led down the hill to Mrs. Quick's. Their feet disappeared, then their legs, then their torsos. Before they vanished altogether, Ben looked back, and seeing that Lola was still standing there, he waved.

About the Author

Joan Schweighardt is the author of nine novels, two memoirs, two children's books, and various magazine articles, including work in *Parabola Magazine*. In addition to her own projects, she has worked as an editor and ghostwriter for private and corporate clients for more than thirty years. She also had her own independent publishing company from 1999 to 2005. Several of her titles won awards, including a Barnes & Noble "Discover Great New Writers," a *ForeWord Magazine* "Best Fiction of the Year," and a Borders "Top Ten Read to Me." And she has agented books for other writers, with sales to St. Martin's, Red Hen, Wesleyan University Press, and more.

Prior to *Under the Blue Moon*, Schweighardt's recent fiction includes the Rivers Trilogy—*Before We Died, Gifts for the Dead*, and *River Aria*—which moves back and forth between the New York metro area and the South American rainforests from the years 1908 through 1929. She has also created and co-edited an anthology on the subject of touch featuring contributions from thirty-nine poets and writers, published by the University of Georgia Press (2023).

Acknowledgments

I owe everything to master layout artist/editor/overall book overseer and literary genius C. P. Lesley at Five Directions Press and to super-talented cover designer Courtney J. Hall. These women are responsible not only for the final touches and aesthetics of *Under the Blue Moon* but also for the kind of ongoing encouragement and friendship that make writing and publishing a joy.

For helping me to reshape earlier drafts of *Under the Blue Moon*, I am endlessly grateful to dear friends and fellow authors Damian McNicholl, Julie Mars, Phyllis M Skoy, and Ariadne Apostolou. You are all literary angels and I cherish having you in my life. While literary agent Liz Trupin-Pulli has not been involved in all my book projects, she is always generous in her support of them and in her willingness to answer questions about publishing options and market trends, another friend and literary angel in my life.

Homelessness is a subject I have given a lot of thought to over the years. I have known people who became homeless, and I have known and loved people who got very close to it. In a previous novel, *The Accidental Art Thief* (2015), I wrote about a woman who becomes homeless due to extenuating circumstances. But I guess I wasn't done exploring the topic, because thereafter I found myself volunteering to be on the board of directors for a local homeless shelter here in Albuquerque, where I live. Over time, I left the board and became a volunteer fundraiser for an annual gala event for the same shelter. These endeavors did not put me in touch with homeless people so much as they put me in touch with really big-hearted, uber-compassionate people who have dedicated their lives to finding ways to help the homeless, as well as other disadvantaged communities. In particular, and from our Barrett Foundation days, I want to thank Kathy Fraser, Eilene Vaughn-Pickrell, and Connie Chavez but also all the others who came to meetings week after week to hammer out ways to stretch foundation dollars to be able to provide fresh-start opportunities for the greatest possible number of homeless women and children in our community. To borrow a phrase from Einstein, you folks helped me to "widen my circle of compassion." You are all superheroes.

For all the love over all the years, thank you always to Michael, Adam, and Alex.

Excerpt from *Before We Died*

I t was Clementine, the old Italian hag who passed herself off as a fortuneteller, who started it all. Mum began seeing her regular after Da died, as she purported to know exactly what Da was thinking over there on the other side. How many times me and Bax gave over all our energy trying to make Mum see the hag was only after her dough, what little she had of it. But she would hear none of it. Then one day, after one of their "sessions," Mum tells us Da told the hag—and the hag told her—that we, meaning Bax and me, needed to get away from the docks and have ourselves an adventure, because we were for fair spending too much time being miserable since Da's passing. We knew Da didn't say no such thing, but we also knew he would have said *just that* if he could look down from above and see the sorry state we were in. We *were* miserable. Me more so than Bax because he at least had the lovely Nora to console him. Mum was all for it back then, this adventure idea, when it was fresh from the hag's lips to her ears. Fuck, she was all for it as recently as the day before.

But now here was our ship—all twenty thousand tons of her, double-masted with one great funnel, booming her kisser like the wild sea lass she was—preparing to cast off, and here was Mum, clinging to our shirt sleeves, bawling and keening like it was Da's funeral all over again.

Nora was there too, of course, with her arm wrapped around Mum's shoulders, trying to persuade her to let us go before it was too late. "Just pull away," she snapped at Bax, her ire on the rise. We looked at each other, me and Bax, but we only continued to try to reason our way out of Mum's grip. She was our mammy after all.

Finally her shrieking became a whimper and she let go of us and we kissed her quick and ran like hell. And sure enough, we were the last two to board. By the time we got up on deck and pushed our way to the rail, we were already pulling away from the dock. "There," Bax hollered. He'd found her in the crowd—her yellow dress, her hat that looked like a rose garden planted on a steep slope—hunched over and sobbing into her handkerchief like an old woman as Nora led her away. I thought my heart might break, it was such a sorry sight. But just then Nora—ever the rip—who'd been bent over Mum, consoling her, straightened and looked back over her shoulder, right at us, and flashed her most winning smile, all gums and bright white teeth. I laughed, because at first it seemed she was beaming at me. Then I felt my cheeks go hot. She was beaming at Bax, of course. He was wearing the new black derby she'd bought him to remember her by. He took it off and bowed and she blew him a kiss. Then she turned back to Mum and resumed her caretaking.

Our sea journey took fourteen days. I brought along a satchel of books, and while Baxter was off becoming intimate with the captain, the crew and all of our fellow travelers, I finished off Jack London's *The Call of the Wild,* which I deemed appropriate given our destination. In the evenings, when Bax had knackered himself sick making new friends and it was too dark for me to read (we'd been told not to light lanterns unless it was an emergency), Bax would ask me how my book was going, which was his way of saying he wanted the story in as much detail as I could remember.

We'd established the pattern back when we were kids, because Da didn't give much credence to a boy who spent too much time behind a book, and while I had nothing to lose going against Da's whims—as I was never going to be the favorite anyway—Bax had the nut hand there and he could not afford to lose it. So Bax got the benefit of my hard work; I read and then I summed things up and related them to my brother, enabling him to learn almost as much as me about books without having to actually crack one. It could have been our little secret too, but Bax was too spirited to try to get away with something like that. "My brother's the bookworm," he'd tell anyone who cared to listen. "I get all my learning secondhand from him." Sometimes he'd add, because it made people laugh and also because it was mostly true, "And he gets all his living secondhand from me." The only book Baxter had brought along was an English-Portuguese dictionary, because he was determined to be able to speak to our fellow *seringueiros* (rubber tappers) in their native tongue.

Nora had been in the same room with Jack London just the month before, when she'd gone across the river to Manhattan with her auntie to attend a lecture given by Mary Ovington, one of the leaders in the women's rights movement and a member of the Socialist Party. Nora had come back jazzed, saying she planned to work with the socialists while Bax and me were away, to advocate for affordable housing for the Negroes. My first thought at the time was, *Now, ain't that ironic? Here she don't really even have decent housing herself, her and her auntie.*

Nora's parents, native-born in New York but from Irish Catholic stock like our own, died of consumption when she

was a toddler. All she remembered of them was their cough-
ing, their spitting up of blood. She'd been raised by her Aunt
Becky, her father's sister, a short round woman who never
married, a socialist and anti-imperialist who gave speeches
and rallied workers to fight for their rights, and who often
dragged her niece along with her to secret meetings—*so as to
indoctrinate her*, Mum and Da always said with a good ounce
of scorn. They lived in two tiny rooms in a dilapidated board-
ing house for women on Jefferson Street. Aunt Becky
worked in a garment factory when she was younger—which
was where she first took note of workers' rights, or lack thereof—but now she had enough dough (Mum and Da had always speculated the socialists were paying her a stipend to
keep her gob running) so that she didn't need to work at all
and could spend all her time rousing others to higher states
of social awareness. It couldn't have been all that much
though, that stipend, judging by their living conditions.

We'd been sitting in the parlor that day, listening to Nora
go on and on about how handsome he was, London, how
smart, and how she planned to read all his books, which she
could do easily enough as she worked in a bookstore now
that she was out of school, and she got her books for cost. He
was my man too, London was. Here was a fellow could clean
a clock when he had to but could also write what was in his
head and even what was not. I hoped to do as much myself
one day, maybe writing stories for the papers or for a magazine, so long as I was never chained to a desk in an airless
office where the risks and thrills of a life well-lived could be
denied me. I wanted to ask Nora if he'd talked about his ad-
ventures in the Klondike, but just as I was about to open me
useless gob, in jumps Bax, saying, "This London fellow...
Would you say he's handsomer than me?" Nora stared at him

a moment, her mouth open and her eyes wide, feigning to be aghast he would ask so impertinent a question. But then all at once she'd squealed with delight and leaped off her chair and planted a loud smacker on Bax's cheek and told him no, never; no one was as handsome as he was, except maybe me (and her gaze came sliding my way, leaving me, as always, with my cheeks ablaze) as I had the same genetic coding, if Gregor Mendel with his pea plants could be believed.

While he didn't care for reading, it was Bax who put our plan together, him and Nora. They combed the newspapers and made a list of New York agents and exporters working rubber in South America and wrote letters to a few of them. Or, to be more accurate, Bax dictated and Nora did the writing; neither of us had good penmanship. One agent-exporter, a Portuguese by the name of Manuel Abalo, wrote back, and when he was in New York on business, Bax took the ferry across the river to meet with him. Abalo wanted to meet me too of course, but our boss on the docks, German fellow who Da had had great respect for, said he'd fire both our skinny arses if one didn't stay behind and get the work done.

Nora and Bax were standing at the door when I got in from the docks that night. I had to plow my way through to get inside and out of my jacket. Even Mum was standing nearby, wringing her hands and looking jazzed. Bax had been back from his meeting for a while by then, but he'd made the ladies wait till I got home, not because he didn't like to repeat himself—old Bax never had a problem there—but because he wanted to feed the drama, as was also his way.

"So he says to me," Bax said to us soon as I sat down, referring to this Abalo chap. "How do I know you can do the work? Why would I want to be pouring money into men I have no proof can keep up? I heard longshoremen were a shiftless lot."

Bax took a step back, so that he was dead center in the room, to demonstrate how he answered. With his chin raised, his legs apart, and his arms folded over his chest, he could have been Hercules himself standing there. "Shiftless, you say? Listen here, I says to the old kinker, I could well name some shiftless bods out there on the docks, but me and Jack would not be among them. I says to him, Me and Jack, we've carried sugar, flour, beef and coal, and much more, in crates weighing twice as much as our own woebegone selves on our young backs, and no one ever saw us as much as flinch. Me and Jack have labored in the piercing cold of winter morns, before there was even a glim in the sky, and under the hottest midsummer sun, working sometimes twenty hours straight, doing what must be done to get our ships loaded and out to sea. We have worked with sponges tied over our ugly gobs to keep the fumes from some of them hauls from choking us down. We have worked bruised and cut and oozing pus from the bottoms of our feet. We have worked sick as dogs. We have worked bleeding like goats, me and Jack have. We have forced our big bodies into wee narrow spaces to take on cargo, and we have lifted above our heads barrels that would kill us fast if one of the other macs was to lose his footing. So say what you will about longshoremen, my good man, but don't dare say it about Jack and me, and never say it again in my presence."

Baxter nodded once, to let us know the drama was over for now—though he maintained his heroic stance in the middle of the room. Nora turned to Mum at once, her jaw dropped open with delight. Mum stretched her lips out flat in response, closest she could get to a smile these days. "And what did he say to that?" I asked. My brother could be a doozer when he wanted. I was the serious one, the thinker. Sometimes I found me miserable self with thoughts behind my thoughts. But I could never have come back at Abalo the way old Bax did. And I will not deny it grieved me some to be lacking Baxter's fire.

Bax waited to be sure he had our full attention. "He said, You and your brother, you've got yourself a job."

We all laughed then, even Mum. I got up to shake my brother's hand, and Mum and Nora stood up behind me, just to be nearer.

Abalo would become our *patrão*, Bax explained, meaning he would arrange our passage to Amazonas and provide us with the tools we'd need to get started as *seringueiros*. We would have to pay him back at the end of the first tapping season, but if we did a good job and brought in enough rubber, we'd have more than needed to cover our expenses. Abalo said we might even want to become agent-exporters ourselves after a few seasons of hard work. There was *that* much money to be made in the industry.

We whooped and hollered when Bax was done with his blather, and the three of us—Mum was watching from the entrance to the kitchen by then—began to dance in a circle, our hands on one another's shoulders just as we did when we was wee wild brats. "We're going to be rich!" Bax cried, and he leaned over to plant a smacker on Nora's bobbing cheek. "We'll have ourselves our own business," he went on. "We'll take turns going to South America to oversee, but eventually we'll hire an overseer, and then we'll conduct our business from here. I'll take you to Paris…" (this to Nora, naturally) "…and we'll have tea with your precious Picasso. We'll live here, of course—because if you can't live safe and full on the

Emerald Isle, where better is there than here in Hoboken in the grand state of New Jersey—but we'll have ourselves a swank office on the top floor of a grand building across the river just like Manuel Abalo. Just like him, we'll look out the window and see the Flatiron reaching for the sun each day, making us feel like anything is possible. It'll be a fine life after all."

His "after all" hit me like a bolt of lightning. "I only wish Da was here to share it," I said. I dropped my hands from Baxter's and Nora's shoulders and our little jig fizzled to an end.

Mum sighed loudly and excused herself, and we watched as she disappeared into the depths of the kitchen. Then Baxter laughed. "If the hag is right," he whispered, "Da knows all about it already!"

"The hag's nothing but a hocus, and you know it as well as I do," I snapped at him. "She wants us to have an adventure for fair, but not because Da's spirit said so. More likely it's a plot to get us out of the way so she can glom even more of Mum's money."

"Whatever your mum pays her," Nora broke in in a rapid-fire whisper, "it's a small sum for the hope and happiness she receives in return. Besides, your mum told me Clementine refers to things she can't possibly know, things that were intimate between them two. So there may be some truth to it after all. Consider that. Or at least respect it."

Her eyes flashed from me to Bax and back again. They went a deeper blue when she got beefed. We took the argument no further.

https://www.fivedirectionspress.com/before-we-died

An exploration of the effects of the South American rubber boom of the early 20th century. The action moves back and forth between the New York metro area and Manaus, Brazil between 1908 and 1929. Through the interconnected stories of an Irish-American family from New Jersey and an Amerindian/European contingent in Manaus, the series explores themes of immigration, sibling rivalry, fortune-seeking, love, grief, greed, despair, and redemption.

"Schweighardt's story happened with rubber tappers a century ago; it continues today around oil, lumber, cattle, soy, and the mining of crystals and other resources … Besides being a good read, this is a wake-up call!"

—John Perkins, *New York Times* Bestselling Author

https://www.fivedirectionspress.com/boxsets

9 781947 044357